Winds Through Time

Winds Through Time

Constance Horne

edited by

Ann Walsh

A SANDCASTLE BOOK

An imprint of
Beach Holme Publishing
Vancouver, B.C.

This book is published by Beach Holme Publishing, #226—2040 West 12th Ave., Vancouver, BC, V6J 2G2. This is a Sandcastle Book.

The publisher acknowledges the generous assistance of The Canada Council and the BC Ministry of Small Business, Tourism and Culture.

The Canada Council for the Arts | Le Conseil des Arts du Canada
SINCE 1957 | DEPUIS 1957

Editor: Joy Gugeler
Production and Design: Teresa Bubela

Cover Art: *A Load of Fence Posts* by Lawren S. Harris, 1911. Oil on masonite, 80.0 x 121.0 cm. Purchased with the assistance of past and present members of the Board of Trustees in honour of Michael Bell, Director of The McMichael Canadian Collection, 1981-1986.

Canadian Cataloguing in Publication Data:

Winds through time: an anthology of Canadian historical young adult fiction

ISBN 0-88878-384-1

1. Canada–History–Fiction. 2. Historical Fiction, Canadian (English). 3. Young adult fiction, Canadian (English). 5. Canadian fiction (English)–20th century.
I. Walsh, Ann, 1942-

PS8532.H5W55 1998   C813'.081'089283   C98-900290-X
PR9197.35.H5W55 1998

This book is dedicated to W.O. Mitchell

Table of Contents

Introduction

On a warm spring evening in 1996 I listened as a frail, white-haired man, his wheelchair pushed up against a small table, spoke to several hundred people in an auditorium in Winnipeg. As he talked his voice faltered, but his words were sure and strong. He told of being a child in the 1920s, of being kept out of school because he had tuberculosis which had settled in the bones of his wrist. He wore a protective cage on that wrist, he told us, but it didn't prevent him from spending his days out on the prairies, watching the gophers as they popped up from their homes to stare curiously at him, listening to the harsh cries of the crows. He spent many hours alone on the prairie, the dust and the smell of dry grass thick in his throat, the empty sky arching above, the wind all around him.

In Canada, he said, a young person has "no medieval cathedrals with soaring Gothic arches to comfort him with ancestor echo."

Those words made a great impact on me. In the darkened auditorium I rummaged for my notebook and a pencil and wrote them down. I realized that Canadians do not need to walk on ancient Roman roads or touch crumbling castle walls to reach our past. We hear our 'ancestral echoes' in mountain streams, in rustling prairie grasses, in the songs of our oceans. We hear our echoes in the wind.

When the speech was over the audience stood. They applauded for a long time; many cried. Finally it grew quiet and W.O. Mitchell was wheeled from the stage.

Bill Mitchell knew well the sound of the wind which blows across this Canada of ours. He heard it first, he wrote about it first, that wind which carries in it the echoes of our ancestors, the voices of people long since gone. The contributors to this anthology have also heard that wind and those echoes. These authors wonder at the vast emptiness of the Canada of yesterday, and they write with great empathy about those who were Canadians before us.

The wind blows. Listen. In a small New Brunswick town, two sisters sit in a sunny doorway, whispering stories to a doll with cornsilk hair. The wind changes and, in another century in another province, medals clink together in a duffel bag as a weary father returns home from war to find that his son is no longer a child.

Listen again. A train whistle wails mournfully. From one ocean to the other train tracks stitched Canada together. As this train crosses a high trestle bridge in

Northern B.C. a boy sits on a hard wooden seat, his mind and stomach uneasy, while a fellow traveller tells of the Gold Rush. In another train in Ontario, a young man imagines he hears the crackle of flames engulfing a cheese factory and wonders if he will be able to solve the mystery of how the fire began. Near a coal mine on Vancouver Island, the earth rumbles. An underground rail car moves slowly upwards towards the light where a desperate son waits for news of his father.

The wind blows though the years. It brings with it, loud in the midnight cold, the whine of a bush pilot's engine. The northern lights blaze; there is laughter. As the wind changes, more laughter comes from a tiny community where a solitary family celebrates Hanukkah in the midst of their neighbours' Christmas festivities.

Listen to the wind. Can you hear the music spilling from a Vancouver mansion where, beneath a candle lit Christmas tree, a masquerade party begins? Can you hear the splash as a whale rises from the sea, and two boys standing on the slippery rocks beneath a lighthouse watch in awe? Can you hear, from a burning shed in the Red River settlement, the panicked whinny of a frightened horse as a young Metis girl struggles to save its life and also to change her own?

The wind's power intensifies. The stiff branches of a dying orchard creak; pages flutter as a difficult letter is written to a grandfather in England. Another shift of wind and a harmonica's tune is carried up to a flock of migrating geese, while on the Saskatchewan prairie below an unhappy boy watches, envying the birds' freedom.

It is the wind which turns the pages of this book, releasing the soft voice of a Japanese grandmother as she tells of being imprisoned in an internment camp during the war; the determined voice of young Nellie McClung protesting in Manitoba years before her suffrage debate; the terrified voice of a mother screaming to protect her child from the cougar who crouches in a tree's shadow.

The wind gusts. As it moves across the land and through the decades, we are blown from from island to prairie, from the Maritimes to the far north, from mansions to shacks, from farm to city. We hear shouts of joy, cries of grief, the howls of wolves and the whispers of ghosts.

Listen to the echoes as you read. Listen to the wind.

Ann Walsh, Williams Lake, B.C.,
January 1, 1998

The Writers' Development Trust has graciously given permission to quote from W.O. Mitchell's speech.

The Crosscut
by Lynne Bowen

"What good will it do you to work in the mine, Jamie? Will you tell me that? You'll come home dirty and wet every working day of your life and one day there'll be a cave-in or an explosion and that will be the end of you."

I'd been wanting to quit school and work in the Esplanade Mine in Nanaimo ever since I was twelve years old, but whenever I brought it up, my mother always got very upset.

In British Columbia you're not supposed to work underground in a coal mine until you're sixteen. But if your family needs the money, the boss of the mine will sometimes let you work even though you're not old enough.

It didn't do me any good to remind my mother that Pa worked in the mine and nothing had happened to him. I tried to tell her how useful it would be to have the extra money, but she wouldn't listen. Once I even said that being a miner would make a man out of me, but that just made her turn away in tears.

"The mines have made men out of too many members of this family already—your grandfather, your father, your Uncle Thomas, your poor dead cousin Jack. You'll stay in school, lad, and finish your grade twelve. Then you'll get a job in Mr. Mayer's dry goods store. You'll wear a clean white collar and a necktie and I won't have to worry every time you go to work that you won't be coming back at the end of the day."

Mother never said any of this when Pa was around, of course. She didn't want him to know how much she worried, but I'm pretty sure he knew anyway. So I stayed in school. But on my fourteenth birthday—May 1, 1887—Pa told me he was going to show me what it was like down in the mine.

It was lucky that my birthday was on a Sunday. Sunday is a day off for most miners, so I wouldn't be in anyone's way. Sunday is also when my mother goes to church. Pa and I waited until she'd left so she wouldn't know what we were going to do. Then he filled two little teapot lamps with fish oil, hooked them onto our caps and off we went.

The Esplanade Mine is only four blocks down Milton Street from our house. When we got to the pithead there was a Sunday crew waiting to go down too, but when the cage came to the surface, we all had to wait while a man led two mine horses off.

The horses were going to the company farm for a rest. As soon as they realized they were above ground, they tossed their heads and whinnied. The man let their halters go and they started to run and kick their heels in the air just like colts do.

As we got in the cage I kept thinking about how glad those horses were to be above ground, but then the gates crashed closed and we dropped so fast it drove the horses from my mind until we reached shaft bottom and I got a whiff of fresh manure.

We walked off the cage into a brightly lit cavern carved out of the coal and rock. The smell came from the stables where horses and mules were resting in their stalls.

"I think it's cruel to keep the animals underground," I said.

"Naw," Pa said, "they lead a good life. They get treated better than the men do. C'mon. We're gonna miss the locie."

A string of empty coal cars stood waiting behind the smallest "locie" I'd ever seen. We scrambled into one of the cars along with the Sunday crew and the little engine pulled us into Number One level. The roof was a lot lower there and the only lights were the one on the engine and the lamps we had lit on our caps.

After a while Pa hollered to the driver to stop and we got out. The locie pulled away and we were alone in the Sunday silence. Our lamps cast small pools of light and a strong breeze swept our faces.

"How come I can feel the wind down here?" I asked.

"That's not wind, son. That's the ventilation system. The big fan at the pithead pulls air through the mine to sweep away the explosive gas. It's because of that fan that this new mine is such a safe place to work."

"Does it ever blow your lamp out?" I asked.

"Yup. Does it quite often. But it's not so bad being in the dark. Let's go into this crosscut I've been working on and you can see what it's like." He pushed back a curtain and turned into a side tunnel. Pit props spaced every few feet lined each side of the tunnel and held up the roof timbers. The props looked like the ribs of a skeleton. We walked deeper into the tunnel until we reached the coal face at the end.

"Sit down here against the rib," Pa said as he blew our lamps out. We slid our backs down the side of the tunnel between two props and sat on the floor. I couldn't see anything, not even my hand when I held it up in front of my face. It was very dark and very, very quiet.

But soon I began to hear things: the trickle of water, the tumble of a rock or a piece of coal, the scrabble of tiny feet and then a strange creaking sound.

"What's that?" I whispered.

"Do you mean the rats or the mine settling?" Pa asked. "The mine's a living thing in more ways than one." He laughed. "Why are you whispering? Are you afraid?"

"No, no, of course not," I said. And I really wasn't.

I was with my pa and everything was all right. The darkness was nice, thick and soft like the velvet I'd seen in the dry goods store.

"When can I work in the mine, Pa?", I asked.

"When you're sixteen."

"What if Mother wants me to stay in school?" I said.

"We'll worry about that when the time comes."

"I could be your backhand. We'd make a great team."

"When you're old enough," he repeated. "Until then I've got Ah Ling."

"You work with a Chinaman?" I gasped.

"Chinaman is a rude word, Jamie." Pa sounded mad. "I don't want to hear you say it again. Ah Ling happens to be a very good backhand. He watches me set the shot that blasts the coal loose and then we both shovel it into the cars. We can dig a lot of coal working together like that."

I knew that there were many Chinese men living in Nanaimo, but I'd never had much to do with them. Sometimes after school my friends and I would see them walking back to Chinatown with their pigtails and straw hats. They'd walk in single file and we'd yell, "Single file. Monkey style."

"But what will happen to Ah Ling when I'm old enough to be your backhand, Pa?" I asked.

"By then, he'll be able to set his own shots," Pa said. "That's if the other miners ever let him."

"Why wouldn't they let him?"

"Most of the men say the Chinese are a danger in

the mines because they can't read English," Pa said, "but if you ask me, that's not the real reason. They don't like the Chinese because they'll work for half the money a white miner gets. They think the Chinese miners will soon have all the jobs."

When we got home that Sunday I asked Mother if she knew Ah Ling. "Of course not Jamie. Those people like to keep to themselves. They don't understand us and we don't understand them and as far as I'm concerned that's the way it should be."

That night as I lay in my bed in the darkness, I didn't think about Ah Ling. I was too busy remembering how it had been in the crosscut with my dad, the two of us together, talking in the dark and the quiet.

Two days later, everything changed. On the 3rd of May 1887, Pa was in the mine working the evening shift. At five minutes to six, just as Mother was tying on a clean apron to serve my supper, we felt a dull thump under our feet. Then we heard the mine whistle blowing and blowing and blowing. On normal days it sounds only once at the beginning of each shift, but this time it went on and on. Mother's face lost all its colour. We both knew what the whistle blasts meant.

There'd been an explosion in the Esplanade Mine. Mother dragged me out of the house and we ran down Milton Street, stumbling on the stones, bumping into our neighbours. Everyone knew the news would be bad, but still they hoped that their fathers and sons would somehow have survived.

As off-duty miners streamed by us pulling on their caps and lighting their lamps, hundreds of women, children and old men gathered near the pithead. None of us said a word. We could do nothing but wait. Now and then the cry of a baby mingled with the sputter of machinery or the shout of the pithead boss, but the watchers stood silent.

Fire had destroyed the fan leaving only a pile of twisted metal. We waited and watched for several hours while the rescuers set up a makeshift ventilation system and cleared the shaft so the cage could operate again. Then the bodies, each one on a stretcher, started to arrive at the surface. For most of the watchers the waiting ended shortly afterward, but for some of us it went on and on.

Hour after hour, then day after day, Mother and I took turns waiting by the pithead. Each time the cage rose, the gates would crash open and someone would call out the name of the dead man on the stretcher.

Then on Sunday, May 8th, one of the rescuers told us that thirty-five men—ten Chinese and twenty-five whites—had been found in a crosscut off Number One level. They had survived the explosion and had built a barricade to protect themselves from the after-damp. All mining families know that after an explosion this deadly gas, carbon monoxide mixed with mine air, seeps relentlessly through the mine. A barricade will hold back the gas, but sooner or later, unless help arrives, the good air behind it will be used up.

The rescuers hadn't reached the thirty-five men in time. When the coal company put up a list of names of the dead, Mother said that since I was probably going to be the man of the house from now on, I should be the one to go and look at it. Pa's name was near the top. When I searched for Ah Ling's name, all I found was "Chinamen 107, 128, 136, 90, 93...."

That night I couldn't sleep. I lay awake in the dark and thought about the crosscut off Number One level. I tried to imagine what it had been like for my father and the other men. How long had the oil in their lamps lasted? What was it like to be in the dark behind that barricade knowing they were using up the good air?

When the news went out across the country that 148 men had died in that explosion, many people sent money. Mother got a widow's allowance, but she didn't get any money for me because I was too old. After that, she seemed to forget how important it was for me to stay in school. She went to see the boss of the mine. He said when the mine opened again he would give me a job above ground on the picking tables.

By this time people were saying that the Chinese had caused the explosion. You couldn't get away from the talk. I went to a meeting at Craven's Half-Way Hotel to hear what the miners had to say.

Just about everyone there was against the Chinese, except one man who said they were the safest workers in the mine. But another man demanded a law to keep them from going underground. The boss said there was no reason to believe that any Chinese had anything to do with the explosion, but he finally agreed to take them out of the mine. He tried to make it up to them by giving them jobs on the picking tables and that's how I met Wan Yung.

We were working side by side looking for rocks among the chunks of coal that went by us on the conveyor belt, and we started trying to talk to each other. What came out was pretty funny sometimes, but we got so we could understand. He was sixteen and he was saving money to go back to China some day and buy his own land.

When I said it was too bad he couldn't work underground and make more money, he didn't really answer. Instead he asked me if I'd ever seen how the mules and horses kicked up their heels with joy when they came out of the cage to go to the company farm. "All creature like sunshine," he said. "Wan Yung like sunshine also. Not like dark."

The dark didn't bother me. When I was finally old enough to go down the mine, Mother and I had a big argument. I said that since I was the man of the house and since we weren't making ends meet, I was going down the mine. Ever since Pa died Mother gives in a lot easier about everything. I got a job driving a horse underground.

My horse's name is Queenie. I hitch her to a loaded coal car and get her moving up the slope by talking tough to her. "Come on now Queenie, I'm not taking any of your guff." She leans into the slope and off we go.

Things had been going pretty well until the day when the flame on my lamp blew out. Suddenly the darkness was all about me and I couldn't get a deep breath. I sat down on the rails and hugged myself trying not to think about Pa.

Queenie whickered at me. Her harness rattled as she shook her head and waited for me to tell her what to do, but I couldn't move. The mine creaked and settled. The wheels on the car squealed as they rolled backward a little.

Then Queenie took over. The coal car started to move forward. All I had to do was hold on to the back of it and go along for the ride. Queenie moved faster and faster until I was running to keep up. It was as if she could see in the dark. After a few minutes I started to hear men's voices and see the flicker of lamps.

Queenie and I had only one ambition: to get to shaft bottom. Once she was safely back in her brightly-lit stall, I climbed aboard the cage for the last time and headed up toward the sunshine.

On Manson Creek
by Joan Skogan

Early in the summer of 1925, my father hung a sign saying "Back in Five Minutes" on the door of his feed store in Vanderhoof. He was about to keep his promise to make me sorry I had wasted my time in the Sixth grade. He delivered me to the train station, telling the conductor in a voice I thought louder than necessary, "He's to go to Prince Rupert. Watch him. He can be trouble. His aunt and uncle will meet the train on the coast."

The conductor did not watch me. I couldn't blame him. The train was full of other children travelling alone to Fort Fraser and Burns Lake and beyond, children whose faces, unlike mine, were not still pudgy and pouting even though they were twelve years old, who did not turn green with motion sickness a few minutes down the track.

The man who did watch me, and took notice of my misery, was white-haired and thin and maybe Chinese, I thought, like Mr. Tim and Mr. George at the OK Cafe back in town. He changed seats with me, so I faced the same way the train was going and no longer saw hay fields and trees spinning dizzily backwards. "My name is Sing," the old man said, as he wrenched open the window so a stream of fresh air flowed over my hot face.

"I'm Eddie," I whispered, and we shook hands. He gave me a sip of tea, sugarless but still good, from a battered steel thermos. Oh, he had spent a good life, he said, north of here, and he waved toward the window he had just opened. My sickness began to pass as I listened to Mr. Sing....

Nearly fifty years ago he had walked from the Cariboo gold fields into the country north of here following a mule, he told me as the train slowed for Fort Fraser. He made me laugh when he hunched over to show how the mule, packing frying pans, flour, pickaxes and other gear had been as old as he was now. He walked north from Barkerville spending the last of his money on that old mule and a prospecting outfit, Mr. Sing said. There was nothing else to do. Earlier, he had paid his wagon fare, and jolted his bones over the new Fraser Canyon road to the Cariboo Gold Rush for nothing. The gold there was gone.

I was certain the same thing would have happened to me. I would probably be failing grades and having to repeat them, or getting places after the gold was gone for the rest of my life. Cigar smoke began to rise from the cattlemen playing poker at the back of the car. I swallowed hard. Mr. Sing edged the window up a fraction more and I put my nose into the opening, breathing in the clean smell of alder and poplar and evergreen trees so thickly grown together they were a green wall beside the train.

Mr. Sing did not seem big enough to have made his way alone through the bush. Maybe he had been bigger when he was young. Now he was watching a clear, fast river running under the railway bridge we were crossing. He did not look as if he were remembering hard times.

The good life started once he got to Manson Creek, Mr. Sing said, sounding happy just to say the words. With a thick-leaded carpenter's pencil, he made a rough map on the back of his ticket to show me Manson Creek, far to the north of Fort St. James, across the Nation River, up in the Omineca country. A long way, and a lot of work, but a good life. And he did find gold.

The first winter was hard. He only had time to stake his gold claim and build a lean-to before the snow fell. Takla Lake trappers and hunters along the trail had warned him the cold would go down to forty below, but still he was surprised how much daylight he burned endlessly chopping wood, cooking (mostly pancakes at first) and washing clothes instead of working his gold claim. In the spring, he set out for Fort Babine.

Mr. Sing's soft voice mingled with the rattle and roar of the train. The rocking motion of the rail car had become familiar, even restful, to me and before I knew it, Mr. Sing had registered his gold claim with a government man named Billy Steele and was back on Manson Creek with Emma, a Carrier woman from Fort Babine.

I remember how he smiled, saying her name, how he tried to convince me I could get off the train for a moment or two to stretch my legs at Houston station. But I was afraid to leave my seat, fearing I would never find it again, or that the train would go without me. Mr. Sing got out at Houston alone and disappeared into the cloud of hot dust drifting in our window. I thought I would never see him again, would never learn what happened next, but just in time he was back, bearing two bottles of orange soda still dripping with ice chips.

Emma was a good woman, Mr. Sing said, and she had her own trapline. I could not imagine my mother in her apron or her church gloves setting traps, but Emma did, and skinned out and stretched and sold the furs too.

The two of them were happy on Manson Creek for years, for many years, for very many years. Then a long silence came between them, as it came to Mr. Sing and me, leaving only the rolling, rattling sound of the train. The old man looked sad and smaller than ever. I did not want to hear what happened next, but the story had become part of our ever-onward journey, and after we crossed a river Mr. Sing called the Telkwa, he continued his tale. Emma cried one day, he said, and told him she knew he wanted to go back to China to die. Go, she said, and I will go back to my people at Fort Babine.

Mr. Sing went to the bank and took out the gold, poured it into a heap of nuggets and dust on a blanket, then divided the pile in half with a stick. Emma sewed little buckskin bags for each of them to hold their half of the gold. He took her to Fort Babine and shortly after, he, too, left Manson Creek. When he got off the train in Prince Rupert, he would catch the Union Steamship down the coast, then board one of the Empress ships in Vancouver for the voyage home to China.

"Was she really your wife?" I asked. Mr. Sing laughed. "More than forty, maybe almost fifty years...that's a wife," he answered.

"And was there really a bank way up there?" Mr. Sing laughed again. A clay bank on the creek, he meant. A good hiding place for gold. No one passing by had ever suspected.

"Smithers next," the conductor called, and the train began to slow. Mr. Sing leaned over the window opening, watching and watching as we came into the little town. I didn't know why. You can't see Fort Babine, or even Babine Lake from Smithers. He sat back and reached out to shake my hand. His was warm and dry and stronger than I remembered from our first handshake. "Goodbye, Eddie," he said in his soft voice. "Keep going. You will have a good life too." He was gone so quickly and completely that I continued to stare at the empty seat across from me for a moment.

Then I understood. Of course. He had changed his

mind, was going back to Manson Creek. I wanted to go too. Mr. Sing would understand, even if my father would not. I ran to the door at the end of the rail car, and jumped down to the station platform, all worries about finding my seat again, or the train leaving without me forgotten.

Mr. Sing had disappeared. No one was at the station but the trainmen checking the couplings between the cars, and a young Chinese man, slim and dark-haired, running as fast as he could go in his old-fashioned boots toward an Indian girl waiting at the far end of the platform. All I could see clearly of her were her outstretched arms. I knew these two had not been on the train with us, nor had they been waiting on the station platform. I turned in confusion, still looking for my Mr. Sing, but there was no trace of him. When I looked back towards the young couple, they, too, had vanished, already on their way back to Manson Creek, I suppose.

I found my seat again with no trouble. My aunt and uncle met the train in Prince Rupert. The summer under their watchful eyes finally ended. Even the following school year back in Vanderhoof finished at last, letting me into the seventh grade. In time I learned to keep following the mule when there's nothing else to do, looking for gold of whatever kind, and a good woman, along the way. Mr. Sing's prediction about my life came true. I imagine he is still up there on Manson Creek with his Emma and his own good life.

Measuring Up
by Joan Weir

Josh stood in the cottage window and stared out. Less then thirty miles away lay the rich grazing fields around Kamloops, but here in Walhachin nothing could be seen but desert and wind and dying orchard trees. His thoughts, however, weren't on the dying trees. They were on Grandfather's letter folded deep in his pocket.

He'd read and reread it till he knew it by heart, but he hadn't answered. At first he'd pretended he couldn't take time to write letters till they'd mended the mile of water flume that had been washed out in that freak spring storm, but that was just an excuse. Three dozen women and a few boys couldn't resink the dozens of huge log supports that had been washed right out of the ground. The flume would have to stay broken until the war ended and the men came back to fix it.

The letter had arrived from England two weeks ago,

dated March, 1917. "I've just been notified that your uncle has been seriously wounded," Grandfather wrote in his usual blunt style. "He's in a field hospital. The doctors aren't sure they can save him. I'm making arrangements for you to come back here and live with me. Meantime, it's important that I know if your uncle measured up out there at Walhachin."

Uncle Trev—seriously wounded—dying maybe....

For the first few days after the letter arrived that blunt fact was all Josh could think about, then the rest sank in. Grandfather was sending for him, but first he wanted a report—but not on the numbers of trees planted or on the bushels of apples sent to market.

Seven years ago when they were still in England, shortly after Josh's parents had been killed in a carriage accident, Grandfather had summoned Uncle Trev to his house in London.

"When you set off for Walhachin," Josh heard his grandfather say as he ushered Uncle Trev into the library, "I want you to take the boy with you."

Josh had been too stunned by Grandfather's words even to move, but Uncle Trev's protest had carried clearly out to the hall. "No way! He's only nine years old!"

"That can't be helped. You're the only family he has left."

"He has you. You're his grandfather. Let him stay with you."

"I'm too old."

"Well, I won't take him. I've waited years for an

adventure like this to turn up. It's my chance to make something of myself, and it will be ruined if I have to drag along a snivelling nine-year-old."

"It could be his chance too," Grandfather added quietly. "Besides, you're in no position to refuse. Not if you expect me to put up the money to finance this adventure."

"But it won't be an adventure if I have to take him with me. He won't get anything out of it and neither will I."

"Then it will be your fault, not his," Grandfather replied. "It's up to you to make sure you both do get something out of it."

"How!" Uncle Trev's anger had exploded.

Until Grandfather's letter had arrived Josh had completely forgotten that conversation. Now he realized that what Grandfather was really asking was whether or not Uncle Trev had made their adventure successful.

Josh's fingers squeezed the letter in his pocket into a tight ball. How could he tell Grandfather the truth without hurting him?

The best thing, he decided, would be to tell Grandfather about Walhachin and let him make up his own mind.

He'd start with the day they arrived.

It had been mid July. The trip had seemed endless, first across the Atlantic, then all across Canada, but at last the train pulled into Walhachin station. He'd rushed to get off, then stopped in dismay, staring at the brown, parched fields and sunburned hills—recoiling from the smothering blanket of heat that made breathing almost impossible. Not a bird anywhere, not a foraging gopher or marmot. The only movement apart from the illusion created by the heat haze itself was an occasional whirlpool of dust set in motion by a gust of wind.

They couldn't be going to live here! Uncle Trev had paid for prime orchard land along the banks of the Thompson River. Instead they'd been given dry sage-covered fields high up on the benchlands more than a thousand feet above the level of the river. No one could grow fruit trees without water!

"Uncle Trev, let's go home!"

For a minute he'd thought his uncle was going to agree, for he looked equally numb and shaken, but the next second he was grinning. "Where's the satisfaction if it's too easy," he said. Picking up their suitcases, he moved along the platform and started talking to the other men about what they should do first.

Josh was too stunned to do anything but follow. He wished his grandfather were there; he'd have insisted that they turn around and go back to England. Uncle Trev didn't know the first thing about planting fruit trees, and neither did any of the other men. They couldn't plant an orchard in this desert!

But instead of going back home Uncle Trev and the other men worked themselves almost to death clearing sagebrush from all the fields and planting five thousand acres of fruit trees. Then, since they couldn't get water up from the river for irrigation, they brought it down from the highest hills by building twenty miles of hollow wooden trough to carry it.

That first summer of 1910 they also built themselves tennis courts, made a golf course, and cleared a field for polo matches. Then they decided to organize fox hunts, using coyotes as substitute foxes. Josh was delighted. He'd never seen a coyote until they'd come to Walhachin and he hated them. Each night at bedtime he refused to go out alone to the outhouse because he could see the coyotes' yellow eyes as they paced along the hillside and he was sure they were waiting to pounce on him. He hoped dozens of coyotes would be killed as proxy "foxes," and listened in glee as the men arranged for a neighboring rancher to catch some coyote pups.

Then Uncle Trev volunteered him to be coyote keeper. Uncle Trev knew how he felt about coyotes, yet he was expecting him to go each day to the neighbor's ranch to feed, water, clean up after and generally be responsible for them.

Not only did Uncle Trev expect it, he insisted on it. For days Josh wouldn't go near the mother coyote and her pups. At feeding time he stood back and threw in the food, not caring if it went in the pen or not, and he pushed their water pan in and out under the wire with a long pole, spilling most of the water.

Then one day as he approached, one of the little coyotes ran to the fence to meet him. Josh stopped walking. The little coyote's tail began to wag.

Next day Josh placed the food in the dish instead of

throwing it and pushed the water dish carefully under the wire with his fingers.

A week later he let the little coyote out and played with him in the yard.

At the end of the summer the men announced the first hunt. Josh's coyote was selected to be the fox.

He watched in horror as the rancher put the little pup into the truck and started off for the hills to set him free. He knew the huntsmen and their dogs would be waiting. What chance would the inexperienced little coyote have?

Josh was too sick and unhappy to go home.

Half an hour later a small grey animal raced toward the ranch yard. Next moment the coyote pup was jumping all over Josh and licking his face. Josh swept him up, hugged him, then put him back in the pen with the others and quickly closed the barn door before the rancher returned.

At supper that night Uncle Trev announced that the men were disgusted with their wasted afternoon and were staging no more fox hunts.

"What about the penned coyotes?" Josh asked quickly.

"The rancher plans to kill them. He says he couldn't trust them not to come back looking for food and kill his chickens." Uncle Trev was watching Josh from under half lowered eyelids. "It's too bad," he went on, "but it's not our affair, so there's no point in fussing about it."

Josh waited till dark, then stole back to the rancher's barn.

"Where've you been, boy?" Uncle Trev demanded when he returned home.

Josh straightened his shoulders and met his uncle's glance. Though it would probably mean a licking he admitted bluntly, "Setting the coyotes free. You said it wasn't our business, but they've got a right to live too."

For a second he thought he saw the hint of a smile pull at his uncle's lips, but he must have been mistaken for the next moment Uncle Trev was pointing at the clock and ordering him to bed.

Also, that first summer of 1910, in addition to their twenty-mile wooden flume, their tennis courts, golf course and polo field, the orchardists built a ferry that could carry messages and equipment across the fast moving Thompson, for their orchard fields lay on both sides of the river and there was no bridge. But the ferry was too dangerous to use when the river was high or when the wind churned the water into rough waves. An alternate method for carrying messages or equipment had to be found. Accordingly, they suspended a large wicker basket on a rope pulley, stretched it from the high orchard fields on one side of the river to the equally high fields on the other, then decreed that the boys would take turns being messenger, as the rope might not support the weight of a man.

It was a scary ride. The unavoidable slack in the rope allowed the basket to drop from the high benchland shoreline on one side down almost to water level in the middle of the river, then to swing back up 1100 feet in order to touch ground again on the opposite shoreline.

Josh was only nine, but Uncle Trev insisted he take his turn with the other boys. At first he was too terrified even to scream. As the high winds rocked and swung the basket he was sure it would upend, or that the rope would break. He clung to the sides till his fingers bled. When he finally reached the other side he threw up.

After half a dozen trips he stopped throwing up. After half a dozen more he stopped being scared.

During the next two years, despite the inexperience of the orchardists, their hard work began to pay off. It seemed the trees liked the heat, and the homemade wooden flume brought down all the water they needed. In both 1912 and 1913 Walhachin fruit was packed and shipped to markets all across Canada. Then came the summer of 1914. War was declared. Immediately, the men began making plans to return to England to enlist.

Josh was then thirteen. "Don't go," he begged his uncle. "What will happen to the orchards if you do? Besides, I can't stay here alone."

"You won't be alone. I've arranged for you to move in with your friend Billy and his mother. As for the orchards, they'll be fine. I'll only be gone a few months and during that time you boys can look after the fruit trees."

Josh felt his panic rising. "You promised when we came that this would be our adventure."

Uncle Trev's face softened. "It has been," he answered softly. "A wonderful adventure."

"But it's not finished!"

"No," Uncle Trev had agreed. "But sometimes adventures have to be set aside if there are more important things that need doing." He'd smiled. "We'll have the war won by Christmas, then I'll be back and we'll finish our adventure."

That had been three years ago, and the war still showed no signs of ending. Uncle Trev hadn't come back to finish their adventure, and now it was too late. Uncle Trev was wounded—dying maybe—and the trees would soon be dying too, for a sudden spring flood had washed out the flume so no more water could come down. It had all been for nothing.

But how could he tell Grandfather that without hurting him?

"Where's the satisfaction if it's too easy?" Uncle Trev's words surfaced unbidden in Josh's thoughts. "It has been a wonderful adventure, but sometimes adventures have to be set aside."

Everything shifted. It was as if Josh had been looking through the wrong end of a telescope. Things that had seemed pointless and stupid before suddenly burst into focus. He knew the answer to Grandfather's question. It had been there all along, only he hadn't been able to see it.

Relaxing his grip on the crumpled letter in his pocket, he reached for a piece of paper from the desk.

"Dear Grandfather..."

A Hero's Welcome
by Barbara Haworth-Attard

I left a pail of milk cooling in the summer kitchen for Ma, scraped a chair up to the table and began loading my fork with scrambled egg. Food half-way to my mouth, Jenny began shrieking, "There's a strange man coming up the lane, Ma!"

We all rushed over to the window, Ma, Harry and I, and peered out over Jenny's brown curls.

"That's no man, that's your father," Ma said. She drew back slowly from the window, her face working, deciding its expression. She quickly crossed to the stove and broke three eggs into a bowl. "Thomas. Pour your father some coffee," she ordered, beating the yolks streaky yellow into the clear whites.

And that was it. No band, no marching parade, just my father walking down the rutted lane in the cool dawn.

I was barely eleven when he left our farm west of London, Ontario, in 1941 for the war in England, and a man of almost fifteen when he returned in late November of 1945.

I poured a second cup of coffee and shoved it across to my father sitting opposite me, in the chair I'd sat in for the past four years. He was shorter than I remembered, but that could be because the years had left me several inches taller.

Ma slapped more bacon on his plate and he nodded his thanks and suddenly it was like he'd sat there every morning. I opened my mouth to ask a question, but Ma shook her head in warning and I stayed quiet.

Harry and Jenny stared at him until I began to wonder if he'd think he'd grown a third arm or something. Harry was five when Dad went away and Jenny nearly two. She thinks she knows Dad but she really only knows him through our stories.

Finally he pushed his empty plate away and stared at each of our faces in turn. "Is it the weekend?" he asked. The first words out of his mouth.

We shook our heads.

"Thursday, Dad," Jenny said. I could tell she was trying out the word *Dad* on her tongue, seeing how it fit.

"Holiday is it?"

Again we shook our heads. I didn't understand what he was getting at.

"Well then, you're all going to be late for school if you don't get moving."

My mouth fell open. When James McKinley's father came home they had a big welcome back party for him. But our Dad...near four years he'd not seen us and he wanted us out of the house.

He pushed back his chair and stood. "While your Ma fixes the lunch pails, we'll take a walk around the farm, Thomas."

I hurriedly shrugged my arms into my jacket and ran down the porch steps after him. He stood for a moment, perfectly still, looking out over frost stubbled fields glowing amber beneath the slanting, early morning sun. We walked to the barn and swung back heavy wooden doors that creaked their protest.

"Could do with some oil on those hinges," he said.

He stopped to pat a cow on the rump. "All milked?"

I nodded my head.

"You didn't take time to clean the stalls though."

"Harry and I do it after evening milking," I mumbled. I wondered if he remembered my letter to him telling of the last calving and how Ma and I had been up all night.

He walked the length of the barn, leaned over and ran a hand along the blade of the mower. "This here's got rust on it. You have to take care of equipment if you expect it to run right."

Anger flushed my face. I wanted to tell him how I worked late into the night after school all September and October bringing in the oats and barley, mowing the grasses, then doing homework with eyes so heavy-lidded the black print in my textbooks jumped around making it impossible to read. Getting the rust off, well, I left that until winter when things slowed down somewhat. I almost told him this, but Harry yelled it was time for school and nothing was said.

As we walked along the concession road, Jenny told everyone who'd listen how her Dad was back. She used the word Dad so much I began to wonder if she knew any others. Harry tried so hard to be indifferent, but he looked nearly ready to burst and finally did, bragging to the boys walking with us how his Dad would tell him war stories all evening long. I almost told him that I doubted he'd hear a single one but decided there was no point in that. I was glad to see them turn off at the little school and let me walk in peace the rest of the way to the collegiate.

I sat all day staring at blackboards, teachers, ruled paper and ink wells, but not seeing them at all. Instead I saw Dad running his hand over the mower blade, pointing to the barn door hinges and the stalls and remembered the letters I wrote telling him which fields I'd planted, which ones I'd left fallow.

Returning home in the late afternoon dusk, I ran up the lane to the house and quickly traded my school clothes for my working coveralls. Through my bedroom window I saw Ma and Jenny in the back orchard picking the last of the apples for a pie. I clattered down the wood stairs and called to Harry. Rushing into the barn I stopped so suddenly Harry nearly ran up my back. Dad was seated on the three legged stool milking a cow. My job.

"You boys get cleaning those stalls," he said without looking around.

Harry quickly grabbed a pitchfork, happy to be free of milking. He'd always been afraid of the cows and their restless feet.

I stood a moment then said, "I usually milk while Harry mucks out."

"Milking's nearly finished so you both can do stalls today," Dad said.

"But that's how we've done it every day since you've been away," I told him, surprising even myself with the stubbornness in my voice.

"Well, I'm back now," he said.

Slowly I took the fork and heaved dirty straw into a pile. My father had been my hero. His feet confidently walked the furrows, planting, harvesting. His voice was calm as he settled the horses and cows. I'd followed behind, walking like him and talking like him, thinking out the words before speaking. That's how he was and how I wanted to be.

"Dad," Harry said, "What did you do over in the war?"

"Pretty much what every other soldier did over there," Dad replied.

Harry waited but Dad said nothing more. No heroic war stories for Harry to repeat at school the next day.

"James McKinley's father came home with a chest full of medals," I said, voice shrill. "Five in all. He wore them to town one day. He told us that he fought so many Germans he soon lost count."

Dad raised his head from the milking pail without losing his rhythm and looked at me.

I pretended not to see. For once I was not thinking about my words before I spoke. "They had a big party for him when he came home. A real hero's welcome."

Dad picked up the pail and pushed past me into the dairy. Harry and I finished the stalls and took turns cranking the handle of the separator. Cream into one bottle, milk into another.

After supper Ma told me to empty Dad's bag in the summer kitchen so she could wash his things next morning. I pulled khaki shirts and pants from his duffel bag and put his shaving kit aside, then heard a clanking in the bottom. Metal hitting metal. I up-ended the bag and out fell a medal and then another. By the end I counted eight, three more than James McKinley's father. Hanging on coloured ribbons, they dangled from my fingers, one with an oak leaf and two with silver bars over star shaped medals. *Pretty much what every other soldier did.* I stood there a long time holding them, then went into the kitchen.

Dad sat next to the stove smoking a cigarette, Jenny leaning against his leg. After a moment he put a hand on her head, stroking her curls. Harry lay on the floor on his stomach, turning the pages of a comic book while Ma darned socks. It all looked so right, Dad might never have been away.

"Where do I put these?" I asked him, holding up the medals.

Harry's eyes went round. "Gosh," he said.

A shadow passed over Dad's face so quickly I wondered if it were just a trick of the light. "Put them on my dresser for now," he said.

I passed through the kitchen to their bedroom and left the medals gleaming in a puddle of coloured ribbon on the dresser. I turned back to the door and Ma was behind me.

"Some men are just like that," she said.

Later that night after the little ones were in bed, I wandered out to the kitchen and saw Dad standing on the back porch. I pulled my jacket on and went out to the woodbox, piling firewood in my arms. I watched the red end of Dad's cigarette move slowly to his mouth and down again, saw white smoke curl up in the black night and wondered how many cigarettes he'd smoked in how many countries. Lord knows, we'd sent enough overseas to him.

"Had a while in Montreal between trains," Dad said, "so I toured around the city a bit. Couldn't believe the amount of stuff in the store windows. Dresses, shoes, chocolate, meat. Same thing in Toronto and I wondered if those people even knew there'd been a war on. Then I get back here, to the farm, and it's changed. You changed. You grew up on me. Harry and Jenny too. Thought I knew that from your letters, but I was wrong."

I said nothing, remembering the letters from Italy, Holland, France, and Belgium.

"Four years," he said. A match flared yellow, lighting

his face momentarily as he lit another cigarette. "I got a bit of money coming to me from the army," Dad said. "Do you think Austin Taylor would sell us his flatlands down by the river?"

Us! I set the wood down on the porch and turned the idea over in my mind before speaking. "It'd make good pasture for the cows. We could get more stock," I said. I took a deep breath. "We could do with some equipment too. New tractor would be nice." My heart pounded in my ears.

Dad nodded. "Saturday morning we'll speak to Taylor, then go to the Co-op in town. See what they have." He ground his cigarette out with his foot, splashing red sparks into the night, and went into the house.

Grampus
by David Spalding

"Hurry up, Robert!" James' nailed boots clattered up the spiral staircase inside the lighthouse, past white-washed walls which reflected the sunshine beaming through its tiny windows. Robert clung to the rail as he climbed higher and higher, peering cautiously down through the holes in the iron stairs, and listening as the sound of the wind grew louder.

In the tiny lamp room surrounded by windows, James was waiting impatiently, anxious to explain how the apparatus worked. "So that's the new lens your dad brought," said Robert, rolling his Scottish "r"s as his father and uncle did.

"You've been here before?" said James, disappointment in his voice.

"Aye," said Robert. "When Mr. Wells was lightkeeper. Dad takes me on his boat when school's out."

"My dad worked at Chance Brothers near Birmingham," James explained proudly. "He helped make the lens. See how the light will go through the colored glass, and make it flash red, white and green."

He opened the little door leading to the balcony. "Come and see the view," he said, stepping outside.

"I can see all right from here," responded Robert, staying away from the door and concentrating his attention on the snow-capped Olympic Mountains, across the Juan de Fuca Strait.

"Come on, Robert," called James. "You're not scared, are you?" He sat on the rail, seventy feet above the yellow rocks.

Robert slowly moved to the doorway, holding on firmly as the wind tousled his hair.

The waters of Royal Roads spread before them. In the west a naval ship was approaching, smoke from her funnel blowing between the white sails. To their right, a narrow strait defined Fisgard Island on which the lighthouse stood. Here, near the dock, Captain McCracken's sloop *Amelia* was moored, its sails furled. Beyond, dense forest climbed the low hills of Vancouver Island.

"The *Shah*'s coming in on the tide," said James. "If you come round here, you can see where she'll go to anchor in Esquimalt Harbour."

Robert peered cautiously round the bulging windows, and saw the masts of two other naval vessels moored beyond Duntze Point.

James rushed right round the narrow balcony, while

Robert clung to the door frame. "You are scared, aren't you?" said James triumphantly.

"I don't like being up high," Robert grudgingly admitted.

"I love it," James laughed. He leaned precariously over the rail and pointed. "Look, you can see the seals on the rocks."

Without moving, Robert gazed over James's head and pointed into the distance. "Aye, and the grampuses in the strait."

It took James a while to spot the tall black dorsal fins of the whales emerging from the swell. He felt a surge of excitement, but was embarrassed that Robert had seen something he had missed.

"We saw a whale from the ship, coming over," said James casually.

"Aye?" said Robert.

"We passed within half a mile of it," added James. "We saw it blow."

"My uncle Willie would have been after it," countered Robert. "He's come from Glasgow to be a harpooner on a whaler." He ducked back through the door and headed downstairs.

James followed his visitor back inside, took his dad's telescope from the rack and looked at the grampuses again. As he watched the fins emerge, James could see the faint puffs from their blowholes.

After more than a month at the lighthouse James was getting tired of his sister's company, and was thrilled to find a boy his own age on the supply boat when it arrived this afternoon. It was disappointing to find that Robert had been to the lighthouse before and, worse still, Robert had seen the grampuses when James hadn't.

"Me mam says to come for your tea now," called James' sister, Emma, from below. "Or you won't get any," she added mischievously.

Downstairs, the boy's fathers had finished tea and left to check the stores, but Robert and his uncle were still sitting at the table.

"Robert's just eleven, like you," said Emma to James. She and her mother questioned Robert about his home and family in Victoria, while James sat beside Robert's Uncle Willie.

"Have you caught many whales, sir?" he asked.

"Aye, I've been twice to the Greenland seas. Fourteen's my tally so far—but I've missed nearly as many." He laughed, then seeing that James was interested, continued his story.

"When the lookout spies a whalefish he sings out and we scramble to the boats. I was captain of the long-boat," he explained. "Every time she comes up to spout, we get as near as we can, and then try and guess where she'll come up again. When we're close I stand up in the bows with a ten-foot harpoon tied to a line. A big one is three times the size of the boat. Then if I strike true, we're fast to the whalefish, and we get pulled along. Every time I can I stick another lance in her guts, till her chimney's afire—till she spouts blood," he added, seeing James' puzzled expression, "then we have to back off till she's died."

"Doesn't it hurt the whale?" asked James.

"It's nothing but a big fish," said Uncle Willie. "Who cares? If I can get taken on out here I want to try shooting 'em with a bomb lance—I hear that's the new way." He put down his empty teacup and went out.

After tea, the boys went outside. "The wind's dying," said James as they rushed down the steps. They stopped to see their fathers checking the piles of freshly unloaded stores.

"I make it sixteen barrels of oil," said Captain McCracken. "Hey, Robbie. Not enough wind to get home tonight. We'll be sleeping on board. You're on your own till we finish the stores."

Robert led the way to the *Amelia*, and showed James around under the amused eyes of the crew. James couldn't help being interested in the little ship, so much neater and more compact than the big square rigger in which his family had sailed from England.

Below deck, Robert opened the door of a tiny cabin lined with varnished wood, with a tiny bunk over a cupboard, and a single porthole. "This is my cabin," said Robert, waving airily.

Back on shore, James led the way, anxious to show Robert each special place on the island, but Robert didn't seem very interested in the boathouse and dock, the oil store, the chicken and goose houses and the weather station. While James tried to explain how he and his father recorded the rainfall and temperature, Robert chattered away about his life in Victoria.

"A canoe came down from the north," he told James. "They were Natives come to dance in the village across the harbour. They wore big painted masks, and I heard the drumming all night." James, who had seen only a few unobtrusive Natives as he passed through Victoria, was fascinated.

Robert talked about Wong Foon, who cooked and cleaned for his family.

"He lives in a little room behind the kitchen, and he burns funny-smelling stuff in there," he said. "And he never has his hair cut; it hangs down his back in a long pigtail, like your sisters'. Dad says he smokes opium on his day off, but when he took me to Chinatown, we just played a noisy game of dominoes with a lot of wee tiles. He called it mah-jong."

When Robert went to the boat to help prepare the crew's evening meal, James' father called him to help get all the stores under cover before dinner. As James carried sacks of flour, sugar and salt into the kitchen, memories of city life back in England flooded back. Why couldn't he live in Victoria, go to school with Robert, and see exciting sights every day? As Emma stowed bags and boxes in the pantry and cupboards, she did not help his black mood. Not only did she seem happy when he was not, but the music hall song she was singing was one that he and his fellow errand boys had often whistled back home. By the time all the stores were under cover, it was dark.

After supper, while his mother and sister clattered the dishes, James sat at the kitchen table close to the lamp and hurried through his studying. When his father had marked his mathematics and settled down with the month-old magazines Captain McCracken had brought, James thought again of the grampuses. Were whales really fish? He could at least try and find out. He scanned the few books on his mother's shelf: *Mrs Beeton's Cookery Book*, a few novels, and some picture books. He passed over Bewick's *History of British Birds*; and took down *A History of British Quadrupeds*, that was the book he needed. It was covered with marbled paper, and had a scuffed leather spine and corners.

It had always been one of his favourites; many times he had leafed through its woodcuts of bats, dogs, mice and deer. Near the end, he remembered, were the whales; never of real interest in Birmingham, where the only open water was a dirty canal and a duck pond in the park.

In the section headed *Cetacea—Whales, Dolphins* he found what he was looking for. Some naturalists thought of them as fish, even though they "bring forth their young alive," and were formed "like the whole class of mammalia." So that's why some people still call them fish, he thought, even the experts weren't sure.

A woodcut of a black-and-white whale began the

section on the grampus. He searched the text, skipping references to classical authors and foreign scholars and what the author considered "fabulous and exaggerated stories" before he found any useful information about the whales he had seen. "The grampus is extremely voracious," he read, "following the shoals of various species of fish, and...pursuing and preying even upon the smaller species of cetacea." Later, falling asleep to the noise of the surf, he imagined the grampuses he had seen chasing porpoises.

Next morning, a little breeze stirred his hair as James cleaned the glass around the light. He waved to Robert on the *Amelia*'s deck, then snatched breakfast—bread and jam and a cup of black tea.

"Off you go and write down the weather," his mother urged as he finished. "It's time, and your father has been up since six and had nowt to eat yet." As Emma cut bread for her father's breakfast, James snatched a slice from under her breadknife and rushed outside. He slammed the door, and jumped down the steps.

Robert was rowing ashore. "He'll be off as soon as the wind freshens," thought James. It had been fun having another boy for company, and now his new friend was going back to the city leaving James alone on the island.

In his imagination he again wandered the streets of Birmingham as an errand boy. He remembered: the constant to and fro of horse-drawn wagons, cabs and carriages; the foot traffic of labourers and pedlars, businessmen and street musicians; the fights, arguments and accidents. Animals had been everywhere and he had been on friendly terms with a couple of dozen horses and dogs. After school he had played hide-and-seek with the other lads in the gathering dusk.

As Robert came up, James silently offered half the bread, and said, "Come and see if we can creep up on the seals."

Scrambling over the rocks, the little island felt very familiar; there was nowhere new to go. It wasn't fair that he had to live in this tiny space, cooped up in the house with his family whenever the weather was bad, with round-the-clock work all the daylight hours. He found himself wishing for a change, a sign, a promise that there could be something more on this rock than hard work, lessons, and the company of too few people.

They passed the weather station, and headed for the west point, where the seals liked to climb out on of the water.

"There they are," whispered Robert. Grey hummocks of different shades rested on the rocks, so still that they looked like rocks themselves. One young one was lying across a small rock out in the water, its head and tail sticking out at each end. They looked as if they could sleep for ever, but James knew that the rising tide would chase them into the sea soon enough. As the boys approached, one or two seals became restless. James ducked down behind a rock and signalled Robert to do the same.

They crept from rock to rock, putting their feet where their boots would be cushioned with rockweed. As they got closer, they could hear the seals snoring and grunting over the splash of the breaking waves.

Through a gap in the rocks they peered out at the seals again, close enough to see their big eyes and long whiskers. Suddenly, there was a commotion. A couple of seals scrambled out of the water, lolloping like giant caterpillars. Beyond, he caught a glimpse of something moving rapidly behind the rocks. As he grabbed Robert's arm and pointed, a tall dorsal fin came into view—a grampus moving quickly through the water! James and Robert were not the only ones stalking the seals this morning.

Only the young seal sleeping on the outlying rock seemed unaware.

The boys glimpsed the black-and-white body of the whale through the water, then for a few seconds it disappeared, fin and all. Suddenly, the front of the thirty-foot grampus heaved out of the foaming water just beyond the young seal's rock. They caught a glimpse of flashing teeth and a dark eye, and the sleeping seal was gone, snatched in a second.

The boys leapt to the top of the nearest rock, and saw a patch of blood widening in the water. The grampus surfaced, the baby seal in those dreadful jaws. The tall fin heaved out of the water and down again, and with a flick of the tail flukes, grampus and seal disappeared.

For a moment the boys held their breath, then

jumped down and ran back towards the landing. Leaping nimbly from rock to rock, James' mind leapt too. His boring island had produced a sight he could not have dreamed of. The grampuses which he had seen in the distance yesterday really were fierce hunters. The book said that grampuses ate small whales; he now knew from his own observation that they ate seals. Could anything as exciting as this ever happen in a city?

Robert waved goodbye and ran to the *Amelia,* and James heard him calling as he scrambled into the boat. "Uncle Willie, Uncle Willie, there's a grampus. Have you got your harpoon?"

James laughed and raced up the lighthouse steps and burst into the kitchen. His parents and sisters turned startled faces towards him as he shouted "Mam, Dad. You'll never guess what I've just seen. The grampus caught a seal. It's not a fish! It's a clever hunter. It's like *us.*"

The Harmonica
by Norma Charles

Ben ducked into the long weeds behind the barn and fished out his harmonica. Leaning against the worn planks he cupped his hands around it and breathed gently, searching for a comforting melody. He played unconnected notes until he found the tune about yellow evening light of the prairies melting into soft purple darkness of the night, about wind stroking tall wild grasses.

High above the barn, a long V of geese migrating south made black silhouettes against the setting sun which outlined the edges of their outstretched wings with gold. Ben lifted his head and played the tune of birds' honking call, the humming music of their wings beating and gliding on the wind.

Out of the gloom the farmer pounced on him. "Ah ha! So this is where you're hiding, boy!" He snatched the harmonica from the boy's mouth. "Told you I don't never want to hear that racket around here again. Never!" he shouted, spouting liquor breath into Ben's face. "What'chu doin' sittin' around on your backside blasting away on this devil's instrument when there's still a ton of jobs left to be done? You think this doggone farm's gonna pick up and run itself?"

"Please Mr. Wayland. Don't take away my harmonica," Ben begged. "It were my pa's and it's all I got from...."

"So it were your pa's, were it? Well, it be mine now, boy." The farmer stashed the harmonica into his dirty overalls and turned away.

"Please sir," the boy pleaded. "I won't play it no more. I promise. I won't never. I'll keep it right hidden away."

A bag of chicken feed was leaning in the shadows against the barn. Ben tripped over it, spilling the feed onto the dirt.

The farmer whipped around. "Now look what you've gone and done! You pick up every last kernel. We're not wasting one bit. Not with the prices they's charging us these days down at the General Store."

His heart pounding, Ben frantically scooped the grain back into the bag. He felt the farmer tower over him, heard him gulp steadily from his jug. Finally he got the whole sack picked up.

"Now look at all the time you wasted, boy, and my supper ain't even been fixed yet." The farmer took another swig at his bottle and belched loudly.

Ben kept his head down and tried to back away from his angry master, but the man grabbed his sleeve. He yanked him up and cuffed the side of his head.

Ben tried to dodge the blows. Ears ringing, he tripped in the muck onto a broken bottle. The sharp glass slashed through his pant leg and bit into his shin. He cried out at the pain. A mist of tears and anger clouded his eyes. Grabbing the broken bottle he lashed out.

"You stop!" he screamed. "You stop 'itting me!"

He caught the man by surprise. He had never dared talk back to his master before. The man tottered back and stumbled. He fell smack, down into the muck. Hard, knocking out his breath.

Ben hurled the bottle toward his great ugly face.

The farmer bellowed and grabbed his head. Ben saw blood gush from his forehead and stream down his cheeks, between thick fingers. The man's eyes grew enormous with horror.

"Blood!" he screamed. "How dare you strike at your elders!" He lunged at Ben, cursing him, his face blotchy with rage.

Ben scrambled out of his reach and fled.

The farmer grabbed up a pitchfork and came after him.

Past the barn Ben raced, darting out into the fields, to the drainage ditch, to the tangled bushes. He dove into the thicket and scuttled between close growing willows, digging his toes into the mud, clawing past the thorny branches, scrambling along a narrow rabbit path, working his way deeper into the thicket's protective shield.

The farmer was just behind him, thrashing ever closer. Ben could hear him breathing hard and swearing at him. "Where've you got to, boy? You jus' wait 'til I get my hands on you...."

Ben's heart pounded like a wild animal caged in his chest. Sobs tore at his throat as he wormed his way deeper and deeper into the thicket until he reached a spot where the willows grew so thickly that even his thin body could not squeeze between the branches. He burrowed into a muddy hollow under a leafy bush and pulled his knees up to his chin. Wrapping his arms around his legs, he curled up into a tight ball. He could still hear the farmer's harsh breathing as he thrashed around the willows.

"I'll get you, boy. And when I do...."

Ben cowered. He grabbed his trembling legs so hard the back of his thin shirt ripped. He dared not move an inch.

The clomping of the heavy boots grew closer and closer. He caught his breath. The farmer must be there, right beside him now. Ben squeezed his eyes shut and froze.

The farmer cursed. Ben felt his heel crush the slender willows right by his back.

The heavy boots stepped again. And again. Was the man moving past him now? The clomping and the cursing grew quieter. Yes! He was leaving the bush and heading back to the farmyard. Ben listened hard. The farmer must have given up his search for the moment.

Ben let his breath out with a whoosh. His heart was still pounding. He strained his ears to hear the man slash through the long grass at the edge of the field. He took another deep breath and blew it out. Then he stretched out his trembling legs. Dark blood was oozing out of the gash that had slashed from his ankle all the way up to his knee. Pain from it throbbed through his whole body.

Although he was cold and hungry and exhausted, he dared not leave his hiding place. He stayed there, cowering under the bushes through the long twilight until darkness fell. Why ever had he thrown that bottle? He knew that striking your master, even in self defense was completely forbidden. He had to get away before Mr. Wayland caught him. Mrs. Wayland had died a couple of months before, so now there was no one else to turn to.

Ben thought of how he used to play his harmonica for the farmer's missus, lively dance tunes that made her hands clap. Some evenings she would even dance around their little parlour.

Mr. Wayland had liked Ben's harmonica music then. At least he had tolerated it, applauding at the end of the dance when his missus laughed and bowed in front of him.

She used to tell Ben that he should play on the stage,

that people from far and wide would come to listen to his beautiful music and forget their troubles. "When you're older, we'll send you to a good music school, then you'll become rich and famous," she had promised Ben.

That was before she got the sickness—the terrible influenza—and passed away in a matter of days as many other farm folk had. Ben had heard on the radio that even young soldiers who had managed to survive the Great War had returned home only to fall sick and die from the epidemic which had swept the whole country.

Now Mrs. Wayland wasn't around to stop Mr. Wayland from drinking heavily, during the day as well as at night. He drank his own home brew made in a still under the chicken coop.

"Good strong chicken smell keeps them other smells at bay," he had told Ben, laughing hoarsely.

Under the thicket, Ben waited, huddled in his thin shirt, trembling like a trapped rabbit. He waited long after the farmer had stopped searching the barn and the fields for him, and after he had stopped banging around in the kitchen getting himself a late supper and had finally gone to bed.

Ben crept out of the thicket, and under a huge star-studded sky he sneaked back to the house. He eased open the back door, held his breath and listened. All was silent, so he slipped in through the kitchen to his room which was in a lean-to attached to the rear of the house. He fished his pack from under the bed and jammed in the stash of clothes he used for blankets on the straw mattress. Then he crept back to the kitchen, bare feet skimming over splintery floorboards.

His harmonica. He could not leave without his harmonica. His earliest memories were of his pa playing lively tunes on it for him and his little sister. He remembered that evening three long years ago, just after the Great War had ended, when he was just nine and his pa had brought him to the Children's Home in London.

They had stood in front of the thick wooden door of the big brick building that was to be Ben's new home for the next few weeks. "But do I really got to go, Pa?" he had asked.

"Course, son. This be for the best. They said they would find you a place on a farm somewhere, maybe even in Canada where they'll fill you up with plenty of good healthy farm food and teach you to be a farmer. You'll like it. Farming's the best trade in the world. They'll always be needing farmers the world over. Them's the salt of the earth."

Ben knew his pa couldn't look after him anymore. After Ben's mother and little sister had died, it took all his father's strength to roll out of bed each morning. And since he wasn't working, there were plenty of days when they had nothing to eat but a bit of thin porridge.

Although he didn't want to leave his pa, Ben was excited about the prospect of an adventure in the new country and he secretly planned that he would send for his pa as soon as he could. Three long years of working for Mr. Wayland had caused that plan to fade but he still thought about his pa often and longed to see him.

That last day at the door of the Home, before leaving, his pa had put the harmonica into Ben's hand. He remembered holding it against his cheek, feeling it was still warm from his pa's pocket. His pa had kissed the top of Ben's head then and had gone off into the foggy night. Ben had not seen him again. A few short weeks later he had been shipped across the sea to Canada with a group of other Home children and taken in a train all across the huge country to the town of Oxville, Saskatchewan where he had been met by Mr. Wayland and brought to his farm in a buggy pulled by an old grey horse.

Ben shook himself. His pa's harmonica. He must find it.

He slid his fingers into the wide drawer in the kitchen sideboard. His harmonica was not there. He hunted above the mantle behind the pot-bellied stove, fingers gliding over the oil lamp, a tin of matches, some thick greasy candles. He probed into a wooden box trailing sticky cobwebs. His searching fingers could not find the harmonica anywhere in the dark room. He didn't dare light a candle and chance waking Mr. Wayland.

The old man must have locked it away in his bedroom, he decided. Maybe it was still in his pocket. Ben could not go to the bedroom. Even when the farmer was drinking heavily, as he did every night now, he slept as lightly as a nervous barn cat.

Ben did not want to leave without his pa's harmonica; he didn't dare wait until morning. He knew the farmer's wrath would not be any less then.

He quickly loaded as much food as he could from the littered kitchen counter into his pack. A hunk of stale bread, an onion, a couple of raw potatoes, a ham bone with some gristle clinging to it. He grabbed the long sharp kitchen knife as well. Just in case.

By the back door he crammed his bare feet into last winter's boots. The soles were worn through and his toes were jammed up against the ends, but with winter coming, the ground was growing colder every day and tight worn-out boots were better than bare feet.

He took one last look around the kitchen and then he melted out the back door into the darkness of the night wind.

If the farmer went into his room as he sometimes did in the night, he would discover that Ben had been back for his pack and would be after him in a flash. He would probably even contact the authorities. Runaway Home child, he would report. Then they would all be after him.

Ben hurried across the cluttered farmyard, keeping low, past the pump house, the pigsty. He tripped on a root and fell against the chicken coop, waking the nervous chickens inside to noisy squawks.

He caught his breath and glanced back at the house.

No flicker of light from the bedroom window. He turned and dashed through the spiky grass into the fields. He ran and ran until his breath tore at his throat, his heart pounded, his sides ached and he could run no more.

The farmhouse was way behind him now, almost out of sight, its jagged black outline blurred into the darkness of the sky.

Ben did not know where he was going, only where he was leaving. He was leaving old man Wayland once and for all. And he was never going back.

He took a good deep breath. Then he straightened up his back and started whistling a tune. It was one of his pa's tunes, a tune of freedom. He stared up into that dark velvet sky and turned to follow the path of the geese across the fields. He headed south.

The Scarlatina
by Joanne Findon

Before the summer of the scarlet fever Alice thought
Mama was always right. About the water cure. About
God. About everything. But then the scarlatina came to
Whittier's Ridge.

The scarlatina had been making the rounds of
homes in the New Brunswick community for weeks,
and now it was high summer. Everyone with hay to cut
was out in the fields. All the children trooped off to pick
blueberries, and often Alice went with them. But this
summer there was no joy in these outings. So many had
been sick, and some children had died. The warm
breezes seemed laced with fear.

Alice sat across from Papa at breakfast. Next to her
was Albert, with Sandy across from him shifting restlessly
on the wooden bench. Beside Sandy sat Frank,
absorbed in a string game. On Alice's other side was

Clara, just turned three, a golden-haired little fairy with a mischievous grin.

"I'll go over to Nancy's this morning," announced Mama as she spooned out the porridge. "She's in mourning for her little Lizzie, who died last night."

"Scarlatina again?" Papa frowned as he bounced baby George on his knee.

Mama snorted. "So they'll say, but more likely from the drug doctoring. Old Doctor Smythe was over there, with his pills and poisons."

"Now, Sarah, Doc Smythe is a good man."

"He may be a good man, but he refuses to see the true light of God's will for natural healing. Here it is 1874, and the new progressive medicine is well known. Yet he still clings to the darkness of the old ways."

Papa looked down at his worn hands. "Don't you think you'd best wait a few days before you go over there? That is a house of sickness now, and you'd not want to bring it home to your own."

"Joel, you know very well that the scarlatina need be nothing more than a cold with a rash alongside it. Edwin had it years ago and was up and running around in two days. Besides, Nancy is my dear friend and has just lost her sweet little girl to the stupidity of modern medicine. I must do my best to console her."

"I only think you ought to wait a few days until the disease has left the house," muttered Papa, "until they've boiled all the clothing and bedding."

"I am fully armed with faith to resist any of the

Devil's artillery."

Alice gazed up at Mama. There was a light in her tired face, and although she couldn't see any armour over Mama's patched apron, Alice imagined it there underneath her clothes, glowing softly next to her skin.

Papa sighed, as he did so often, and went back to eating his porridge and bouncing the baby.

"Can I come with you Mama?" asked Alice.

Papa's head flew up. "No, Alice."

"But I could play outside with Jeremiah. I wouldn't go in."

"Alice, even a little dog can carry the disease. I'll not have two members of my family taking risks."

Alice glanced over at Mama. She was scrubbing the porridge pot and not looking at them. Papa would have his way in this.

Mama walked out into the hot sunshine an hour later with a loaf of barley bread wrapped up in her apron. Papa had long since limped out to the only field left untrampled by the neighbour's cows to cut hay. Albert had gone with him, and Frank and Sandy were floating twig boats on the pond. Baby George was asleep, and Alice sat with Clara in the strip of sun in the doorway of the house.

"Emily needs new hair," said Clara, combing the corn-silk hair of their one doll with her fingers. The threads were dry and some of them came out in her hands.

"You shouldn't comb it so often," Alice told her.

"But if she's a princess she can't have tangly hair. I'll ask Mama to fix it."

"She doesn't have time right now."

Clara gazed up at Alice and smiled suddenly. "You could fix Emily's hair, Alice. I know you could!"

Alice looked hard at the doll and thought maybe she could. She had watched Mama often enough. And she was the oldest girl, thirteen now. Surely she should be able to fix a little doll for her sister. But she had to ask Mama one thing.

"Wait right here for me, Clara," she said. "Don't move."

Alice wasn't sure why she had to follow Mama right then. The question about how to tie on the corn-silk could wait, and she could fix the doll later. But before she knew it she was running down the path.

The dew clung to Alice's short dress and trousers as she ran along the trail through the fields of tall grasses that connected their land with the McDermotts'. Mama was far ahead, striding along, short hair bobbing as she walked. Her Reform dress and cropped hair made her look so different from the other mothers. Alice and Clara wore the same kind of outfit, but long pantalettes weren't so unusual on children. The boys all wore the same old clothes, but Mama had cut off Alice's long dresses and made pants to go underneath. Mama said the Reform dress was healthy and natural, just as God intended women's clothing to be. But some of the neighbours thought she was crazy.

Ever since Mama had started getting the *Water Cure*

Journal from New York and reading Dr. Trall's big book everything had been different. They never ate meat or pastry anymore and drank only cold water and milk. Mama gave them special baths when they got sick instead of sending for Doctor Smythe. And she always talked about how living this way was God's will. She even said that to people at church, although most of them muttered and turned away. Most days Alice didn't mind it all, and when Mama showed her pictures of the dress Reformer ladies in Boston wearing their bloomers, she even felt sort of proud. Still, Alice was glad she didn't have to go by the McShane place where the boys liked to holler "Trousers! Trousers!" at her.

"Mama! Wait!" Alice called. But Mama was far ahead and didn't hear her.

Alice reached the McDermott's yard just as Mama knocked on the door.

Nancy McDermott opened it, wiping her hands on her apron and looking amazed.

"Sarah Craig! What are you doing here? Aren't you afraid of taking the rash?"

"No," said Mama firmly. "Disease and death belong to the Devil; I do not!"

Alice shivered. For a moment, Mama was a fearless angel, standing against all the evil in the world. She walked right into the house and disappeared in the gloom. Nancy stood frozen in the doorway. Alice saw surprise, then rage wash across her face. And hurt? Yes, hurt. It was there only an instant; then she turned and slammed the door.

Alice stood panting in the sun. She stared at the closed door, wondering about Mama and the fever and the Devil. The house was silent. Alice turned on her heel and ran home to Clara, her question about the corn-silk forgotten.

A few days later Clara pushed her bowl away and laid her head on the table.

"What's wrong, sweetheart?" Mama was at her side with a hand on her forehead.

"I want Alice to eat my breakfast," murmured Clara. Her golden curls were darkened and plastered to her head.

Alice sucked in a quick breath. Fever.

The red patches appeared on Clara's skin a couple of hours later. By then she was in bed, stripped and covered up to her chin with a light cotton sheet.

"Can I help tend her, Mama?" Alice asked.

Mama nodded. "It's time you learned the proper treatment of a fever. First is the wet sheet pack."

Mama wrung out a sheet in the basin of cool water.

"Help me wrap this around her," said Mama. "It will draw out the noxious matter in her blood and bring down the fever."

They wrapped the wet sheet, then another dry sheet, around Clara's shivering body. The girl whimpered once, then lay silent.

"We'll leave her in these for a couple of hours," said

Mama. "Meantime, bathe her face and neck with the cool cloths."

Alice sat there all day, wiping Clara's hot face and coaxing her to drink sips of water. Late in the afternoon, she helped Mama replace the wet sheet with another. This time Clara didn't make a sound. Alice stared at her in alarm as Mama drew Clara's limp arms inside the new wet sheet.

"Don't be afraid, Alice," said Mama. "This deep sleep will refresh and heal her."

Around suppertime Frank came in and flopped down on the threadbare rug in front of the stove.

"My head hurts," he said, and fell asleep right there on the floor.

"May the Lord help us all," sighed Papa.

The next morning Albert was sick, his face and arms bright red with the rash. By noon Sandy was down with the fever too. Frank didn't seem too bad, but Clara's face had swelled up and she looked like a bullfrog with bulges underneath her ears.

"Is she going to die?" Alice asked Papa.

"No, pet," he said, squeezing her shoulder. But Alice thought he didn't sound too sure.

"We're following the most up-to-date treatment set out in *Dr. Trall's Hydropathic Encyclopedia*," said Mama. "Dr. Trall has never lost a patient to scarlet fever."

Alice bathed Clara's face and throat every few minutes. But no matter what they did, her skin was as hot as ever. Why wasn't the water treatment working?

Alice sat with Clara until her eyes hurt and her head drooped. Papa picked her up and tucked her into the daybed across the room.

On the fourth morning Alice woke with a blinding headache. She tried opening her eyes, but even the dim light from the cabin's one window seemed fearfully bright. Closing her eyes to slits, she rolled over and slipped out of bed. A wave of dizziness slapped her on the head.

"Mama!" she cried.

Mama's arms folded themselves around her and lifted her back into bed. She looked up into Mama's tired face.

"Mama," she whispered. "I can't get sick! I have to tend to Clara!"

"Hush now, darling. Papa and I will manage." Mama said with a sigh.

Alice drifted in and out of sleep. Days went by, maybe weeks; she couldn't tell. Sounds came in waves: Papa's soft voice, the tinkling of water in the basin, baby George's cries, Mama scrubbing dishes in the night, Papa's snores. Sometimes she woke to find Mama or Papa bathing her hot skin with water, and tried to smile. One day she thought she saw Frank and Albert making buckwheat cakes for their supper. They must be better, she thought. Mama was right; the water cure really was the best treatment.

But one afternoon she heard Mama and Papa talking in low, pinched voices.

"It is my own fault," Mama said. "It was pride rather than faith that drove me to visit Nancy so soon. It is my own folly that brought sickness into this house."

"What's done is done," said Papa. "We can only trust our Heavenly Father now."

"I cannot understand it. Dr. Trall writes in his book that he has never lost a patient...."

"Dr. Trall is in New York, Sarah. He has a clean, bright clinic and plenty of good food. He is not a crippled man scraping a living out of the New Brunswick wilderness, pinching out a few grains of corn and barley for his starving children...."

"Now, Joel...."

Alice tried desperately to listen. Which patient was about to be "lost"? She tried to use her fear as a rope to pull herself back, but soon drifted away again.

The next morning Alice's headache was gone. She climbed slowly out of bed and stumbled to the far corner where Mama sat slumped beside a figure in the bed.

"How is she, Mama?"

"It has been a hand-to-hand struggle with death from the start. The disease went to her ears and she is almost deaf, but she spoke to me once this morning and seems better."

Alice leaned closer. Clara's rash had vanished but her hands were moving slowly, scratching her head. Alice watched the little fingers close around a clump of golden hair and pull it out. Clara laid the hair on her chest and lifted her hand to her head again. Mama grasped it gently and pulled it away. Clara's eyes opened and she stared first at Mama, then at Alice.

"Are you thirsty, Clara?" said Alice.

"No." The voice was thin but clear.

"You're going to get better now, aren't you?" said Mama.

"No."

Alice leaned forward. The bulges around Clara's throat and ears were gone, but her eyes looked far away as if she didn't really see her or Mama at all.

"You have to get better, Clara," Alice said as a coldness closed around her heart. "Remember our stories about Emily? You've got to get better or Emily will be lonesome."

"No."

"Come now, Clara, you're not going to leave us, are you?" asked Mama.

"Yes."

"No, Clara! I won't let you die!" Alice grabbed Clara's hands and shook them.

"Hush now, Alice!" Mama said, drawing her away. "Pay her no mind; she doesn't know what she's saying. Her fever is gone and she is certainly getting better now."

But as Alice watched by Clara's bedside that day, she grew certain that Clara was already walking in a different world. Although her eyes stayed open and bright, they didn't seem to see the unfinished wooden walls of the cabin or any of the worried faces that bent over her. Alice gripped her small hand and told her the Emily stories one after another. But even the one about Emily lost in the woods didn't pull Clara back from wherever she was.

Around midnight, Alice woke from a deep sleep to the sound of sobbing. She sat up. It was Mama. She had never heard Mama cry before. She leapt out of bed, shaking all over.

"She's gone." Tears streamed down Mama's face.

Clara's little face was calm, her far-seeing eyes closed. Papa held her still hands in his.

"She looked into a world where there is no sickness, and knew she was going there to stay," sobbed Mama. "Oh, if only I had listened to you, Joel!"

"No!" cried Alice, backing away. She felt as if her chest would burst. She yanked the door open and ran sobbing out into the black night, out into the darkness where the trees tore holes in the web of high cold stars.

The breezes were cool on the hilltop that Mama called her "flower garden." Here were four small graves: baby Jimmy, smothered accidentally; John Edwin, drowned in the pond three summers ago; a nameless girl, born dead. And now, Clara Matilda, June 10, 1871—July 25, 1874. "In the arms of her heavenly father," Papa had written on the little wooden cross.

Alice came here often. She hated the house with its dirty pots and dark corners. She hated the shouts of her brothers. She hated Mama's quick, busy movements.

Poor Emily sat on the grave among the wildflowers, bedraggled now from the rain and dew. Her hair was even more tangled than before.

Alice knelt in the warm grass and drew the skein of corn-silk from her apron pocket. Carefully she smoothed it out across her knee, then reached for Emily. With the doll nestled in her lap, Alice slowly braided the new silk in with the old. Sunlight glinted on the pale hair and she remembered how Clara's hair always glowed when the sun caught it. Her fingers kept weaving, in and out, bright hair and bright memory, until the wind, the sun, the corn-silk and Clara's hair were one, without end.

A Horse For Lisette
by Linda Holeman

It was the crow that woke me, his boastful cry echoing into our sleeping loft. Every day the crow perched on the roof of the animal shed, and as I lay on my pallet, feeling the warmth of the September morning and listening to him, I wondered if I would miss even him when I left.

By this time next week I would be a bride, and from then on sleep in my husband's bed many miles from my home in the Red River Settlement. Tears formed and started down my cheeks. I angrily brushed at them and sat up. What more could I say to Maman and Papa so I would not have to marry Fergus MacDonald? It seemed I'd run out of words. Papa wouldn't discuss it any further, and with Maman it was always the same. I would plead, and Maman's long black braid would sway as she shook her head, her full lips sorrowful yet firm as she spoke in soft Cree.

"You know how proud it will make Papa. You will do fine, Lisette, just fine. You have a quick mind and skillful fingers. It will take a little time, and then you will settle down." Yesterday she had paused after the familiar speech, as if she were about to tell me a secret. She looked up from her stitching, glancing around to make sure we were alone. "And you have a brave heart, my daughter," she whispered. "A good and very brave heart. Not everyone has such a heart." Then she looked down at her needle and thread again, as if the praise were something shameful, as if my heart, hearing about its bravery, might grow large and vain.

I didn't want to think about my heart. I knew that even if at one time it had been plump and red and full of love for my mother and father and brothers, and for our gentle cow and plodding oxen and even for the proud chickens who scolded as I searched underneath them for their eggs, my heart had changed. No goodness lay in the black and withered lump that was lodged behind my ribs; it was full of anger. I could not bear to marry old Fergus MacDonald and follow him to some distant Hudson's Bay trading post. Papa said that Monsieur MacDonald might some day be *le grand bourgeois*—the big boss, in charge of the whole district of posts. Papa himself had once been a voyageur, and had looked with admiration on *le bourgeois*. And now one of them had brought him a sleek and beautiful horse in exchange for me. My marriage would connect Papa to a powerful man.

"Think of it, Lisette," he had said, his dark brown eyes lit from within as he stroked the horse's glossy back. "In these times many fathers must pay a large bride sum to find a husband for their daughter. But Monsieur MacDonald has given this for you, in return for your hand. It is best for you, *ma fille.*"

And for you, I thought.

Fergus MacDonald wasn't as old as Papa, but much, much older than me. His fingers were already twisted from many years of hard work, his back slightly humped. There was no kindness in his eyes. I shook my head to push away the thoughts of the wedding—and after. Only one week ago—September 18, 1832—it had been my thirteenth birthday. I would want to marry someone, someday, but not yet.

Now the crow was silent, but I heard a soft questioning whinny from the shed. I dressed quickly, crossing my shawl over my white blouse and tucking it into my long dark skirt, pulled on leggings and moccasins. I climbed down the ladder, stopped to grab a long, whiskery carrot from the pile on the table, and hurried to the shed.

"*Bonjour*, Fripon," I said to the old horse we'd had for many years. Then, "There, there, little one," I murmured to the new horse standing in the shadows of the stall. Even in the dimness of the windowless shed, I could see that his eyes were glazed with worry.

"I know you feel strange, Billy, away from your home." I undid the rope that held the stall's gate, and slipped in. He shuddered as I approached, but his velvety muzzle stretched and sniffed at the carrot. Almost daintily, he took it from my palm and crunched it. I scratched his narrow forehead and ran my fingers over his long, silky ears. "I'm sorry that you had to leave your home because of me, *petit* Billy." His eyes, calmer now, rested on mine.

"Lisette! Lisette," Pascal's high voice called, "Maman says to come and help her." Pascal was six years old and the spoiled baby of the family. I was in the middle—three boys, then me, then three more boys. Papa always told everyone how he had been blessed— six strong sons. Two were already out in the world, both as engages—canoeman—for the Hudson's Bay Company. "And four more still at home to help me," he would always add.

"Papa says this, Papa says that," I grumbled to myself as I closed the stall. Papa was always telling everyone what to do. Maman didn't mind. Or if she did, she didn't show it.

Papa never boasted about me. Instead, he told me he was sorry I was not more like my mother. He often warned that I would never find a husband, not with my wagging tongue and wild and disobedient ways. So when Fergus MacDonald came calling, after seeing me with Papa at Fort Garry a few months ago, Papa had been all too pleased.

Crossing the yard back to the house, I stopped and sniffed the air.

"Maman," I said, taking a wooden bowl of dried berries Pascal and my two other younger brothers, Bernard and Nolan, had gathered in late August, "do you smell something?"

Maman straightened from the blackened pot that hung in the fireplace, her nostrils quivering. "The neighbours were burning a field yesterday. It lingers." She stooped to stir again. "Papa and Narcisse will be hungry from their trip to the fort," she said. After Papa had injured his back and could no longer paddle, he had begun farming on one of the narrow plots offered at the Red River Settlement. Now he supplied vegetables for the Hudson's Bay Company. "We will let them eat in peace."

I knew she was telling me not to say anything about Fergus MacDonald when they arrived home. I looked around as I ground the berries to add to pounded buffalo meat and fat to make pemmican. Once I left, I might never see this place, or Maman, again.

Sunlight filtered through the windows made of parchment. The fire, fuelled by dried buffalo chips, popped gently in the stone and clay fireplace. A blanket across one corner of the room, attached to the ceiling by *babiche*—the thongs made of strips of buffalo hide — created a sleeping chamber for Papa and Maman. The scrubbed wooden table sat in the middle of the room. I could never remember a time when there wasn't food there, filling the air with fragrant aromas. I realized my eyes were wet again. I closed them to stop the hot ache, and in that moment Pascal's scream, hollow with panic, cut through the quiet.

Maman and I jumped to our feet and ran out the door, holding up our skirts.

The shed was blazing, brilliant scarlet and yellow flames hungrily licking up one wall. Mama grabbed a blanket from the clothesline and began beating at the fire, pushing Pascal behind her.

"No, Lisette, no!" Maman called as I ran toward the shed door. "Come away!" But I didn't stop.

Thick black smoke made it difficult to breathe or to see. I opened the cow's stall, and then the ox's, and shoved them toward the open doorway. Then, pulling my shawl over my mouth and nose, I felt my way to the back of the shed, reaching out with my free hand.

"Fripon! Billy!" I shouted, the hot air rushing into my throat and coating it with dark pain. The smoke was now so thick that all I could do was fumble blindly to find the horses' stall gate. I got it undone, and at that moment the low roar of the fire changed to a sudden loud whooshing, and the flames grew brighter. In the sudden glare I could see both horses. Old Fripon stood trembling, while Billy was backed into the corner, his head thrust up. I took their harnesses and pulled. Fripon came forward, but Billy wouldn't move. He was frozen, terrified of the flames. I pulled off my shawl and tied it around his eyes.

His head immediately dropped, although his sides still heaved, and long strings of frothy saliva ran from the sides of his mouth.

Bending as low as I could, my own eyes and nose streaming, I led the horses outside. Bernard and Nolan had appeared, and were throwing buckets of water against the shed. Maman was still beating at the fire with the now shredded blanket, Pascal crouching behind her.

As I breathed in short, quick gasps around the heat in my chest, I saw the entire wall of the shed and part of the roof cave in. I took my shawl from Billy's head, and he snorted and shook his mane. His eyes rolled once, then met mine. In that instant I made a decision.

"Go home," I said, my voice fierce and harsh, a voice I didn't recognize. "Run, Billy." I slapped him once, hard, on the rump.

Billy reared up, and then, in the next instant, was gone, his hooves thundering across the mossy ground.

We heard Papa and Narcisse before we saw them. The rumble and shriek of the wooden wheels of the Red River cart reached our ears less than half an hour after the rest of the shed collapsed. But we had managed to wet the ground all around the shed and had beat out the last flames so that the fire couldn't spread to the house.

We all turned toward the rutted road. Soon we made out the ox, straining at his leather harness, with Papa standing high, shielding his eyes with one hand. While the cart was still rolling, Narcisse leapt off and raced toward us.

"We saw smoke," he yelled. "Are you all right?"

"Yes," Maman answered. "But the shed is gone."

Papa pulled hard on the reins. He jumped down and hurried to Maman. "You're not hurt, *cherie*? Nor the children?"

Maman shook her head. "It must have been a peat moss fire, creeping underground. It started at the bottom of the shed."

Papa looked at the huge smoking heap of blackened wood. "The animals? Did you get the animals out?" His face was blotchy and pale beneath his dark summer burn of wind and sun.

"Yes," Maman answered, waving her arm toward the animals now tied close to the house. "Lisette did. Lisette saved the animals. Without her...." Maman stopped, then smiled at me. Her slow, tired smile brought a burning, not caused by the smoke, to my eyes.

"But she let Billy go," Pascal said, filling in the empty space Maman had left behind her words. "I saw her, Papa. She brought him out of the shed, and then she slapped him, and he ran away."

I glared at Pascal, but he was grinning up at Papa, waiting to be praised for his betrayal. I was afraid to look at my father, heavy dread pushing low in my stomach. But I put my chin forward and fought to keep my lips from trembling.

Papa stood in front of me. "Is this true, Lisette?"

I looked into his face, but had to wait a few seconds before speaking. "*Oui*. Yes, Papa," I finally answered, louder than I had intended.

Papa continued to hold my eyes with his for a few very long minutes. Then he turned and strode toward Fripon. "I will be back," he said.

"Are you going to find Billy, Papa?" Pascal asked.

Papa moved his head in what could have been a nod yes or maybe just another look at what had been the shed.

"Lisette, go inside and prepare tea," Maman said.

I stumbled toward the house, silently thanking Maman for the excuse to go inside.

I tried to sip the strong black tea, but there was something in the back of my throat, mixed with the taste of charred wood, and I couldn't swallow.

Before darkness fell, my brothers had eaten and silently gone up to bed. Sitting across from Maman at the table, our hands not busy for once, I heard the heavy steps of only one horse.

Papa came in. "Billy ran to his old home." He sat, sighing, and reached for his pipe and tobacco pouch. The flicker from the fireplace danced on the ceiling. "I told Fergus MacDonald that perhaps, since the horse was so anxious to stay at the home he knows so well, that this is not the best place for him after all," he said, busy filling his pipe.

I heard a tiny sound, an intake of breath, from Maman.

Papa lit his pipe and then went to the door and pulled it open. "There will be other horses," he said, and without looking back, walked out into the night.

Higher Ground
by Beverley Brenna

Nellie Mooney dropped her basket of eggs and picked up a stick to chase the speckled chicken to the other side of the tidy, log henhouse. Her usually laughing eyes were wide with anger.

"Stay over there, you bad thing," she yelled, "or I'll put you in the stew pot. Stew pot!"

She turned and examined the yellow hen the other chicken had been pecking. It fixed a watery eye on her as she clicked her teeth at its bald and bleeding rump. Then it bobbed over to where she had dropped her basket.

Nellie checked through the eggs. Two had been cracked by the fall. Eggs were very dear, ten cents a dozen. Her first impulse was to hide the broken ones under the straw, but she wanted her mother to see what that awful chicken had made her do.

"Stew pot!" she hissed at it again. "I should let you out for the weasels." But she didn't. She carefully closed the henhouse door and headed up the hill to the farmhouse where she lived with her parents and five older siblings.

Her mother, however, did not lay the blame for the broken eggs on the chicken.

"Get the churn," said Mrs. Mooney crossly. "You will make the butter."

"But I—" Nellie began.

"Enough," warned her mother. "Do as you're told."

Inwardly, Nellie groaned. She had hoped to spend the morning outside collecting arrowheads among the goldenrod and piles of buffalo bones down by the creek. The buffalo had vanished in 1879, the year before Nellie's family had come to Manitoba. Secretly, Nellie hoped she'd see one of the lost giants after all, maybe among the poplar bluffs or galloping its way north west across the prairie towards the mysterious, blue-black Brandon Hills.

Pushing the handle of the big, wooden churn made her arms ache and as the butter started to form, the foot pedal got harder and harder to press. As she worked, she thought of the First of July picnic in Millford that afternoon, wondering if there'd be chocolates. Someone had brought some to last year's picnic—the first Nellie had tasted—and she had made hers last as long as she could, enjoying the unbelievable sweetness.

Dreaming of the picnic, Nellie missed the rattle of

the small chunks of new butter. Gas building up inside the churn popped the cork and cream flew everywhere.

"Oh Nellie, you didn't let it air!" cried her mother, running in to see rivulets of cream seeping into the cracks of the floor.

"It came too fast," Nellie exploded, much as the cream had done. "Stupid old stuff! I don't know why we need butter anyway—"

"You will learn to hold your tongue, young lady," interrupted her mother. "That is a lesson you seem reluctant to learn, but maybe cleaning up this mess will teach you once and for all. Unless perhaps you'd prefer not to go to the picnic."

Nellie's arms and legs ached, but she went out and got the bucket and filled it with hot water from the stove.

"Hold your tongue, hold your tongue," she thought. "Someone's always telling me that."

As she scrubbed the floor, she recalled the discussion about politics her mother and brother had had the other day. Her brother hoped a young lawyer from Winnipeg would earn a seat in the local legislature, but her mother strongly disagreed with his choice.

"Just vote for who you like," Nellie had said to her mother to calm things down.

"Hush!" her mother snapped. "Women aren't allowed to vote."

"Not allowed to vote!" exclaimed Nellie. "But that's wrong!"

"Hold your tongue," said her mother.

"I'd like to throw this butter out the window," Nellie muttered when she had finished cleaning the floor. Then she smiled in spite of herself. "But first I'd like to churn that chicken into it."

Nellie tipped the heavy churn from side to side until the butter had chunked into one large piece. Then, her thin arms trembling, she carefully drained out the buttermilk and scooped the butter into a wooden bowl where she worked in the salt. Finally, the butter neatly squared inside paper wrappers, Nellie approached her mother.

"Isn't it almost time for the picnic?" she asked carefully.

"Yes, yes, I suppose it is," answered her mother. "Change into your church dress, with the straw hat to match. Your sisters are upstairs."

Nellie looked admiringly at the new print dress she pulled from the closet. Her mother had made it from material she brought from Ontario when they moved three years ago and Nellie was seven. The hat that went with the dress was lined with the same flowered cloth.

As Nellie climbed into the wagon behind her father, she noticed that her brothers hadn't had to change their clothes. Lizzie, one of Nellie's older sisters, carried the carrot gelatins their mother had set overnight in the cellar. Hannah, the other sister, carried cinnamon rolls, curled like snail shells. Their mother held the hamper which contained ham sandwiches, plates, cups and cutlery, with two pies on top. Without fruit or eggs for

the pies, Letitia Mooney had concocted a filling of
molasses and butter thickened with bread crumbs and
flavoured with vinegar and cinnamon. The three boys
didn't carry anything.

Tables had been placed under the poplar trees by
the flax blue water of the Souris River. When the
Mooney family arrived, they added their contribution to
what was already there. Nellie walked along, admiring
the variety. On one table were placed devilled eggs,
buns, slices of cheese, sandwiches, and hard boiled
eggs. There were also plates of fried chicken—although
not Old Stew Pot, thought Nellie regretfully. The next
table held potato salads, cabbage salads, jellied salads,
lettuce cut up in sour cream, and pickles. Then there
were the pies, the doughnuts, the jelly rolls, the cookies.
Large coffee urns stood over to one side, the smell of
the brew better than the taste, thought Nellie. And
there was lemonade in big, metal cream cans.

At a booth set up that morning and run by the
district's welcoming committee, there was fresh ice
cream made by Hettie Smith who had ice from winter
kept in sawdust in an ice shack behind the house. Nellie
had never tasted ice cream and she went over to take a
peek. It looked like custard. The money made at this
booth would go to welcome the new pioneers who had
settled in the area, buying them baskets of supplies
from the store in Millford. The smell of vanilla made
Nellie's mouth water.

"Five cents a bowl," said one of the women running

the booth.

Five cents! Nellie swallowed hard and thought of those broken eggs. She couldn't ask her mother for money now.

Instead, she got a plate and helped herself to the food on the tables. She didn't take any of her mother's sandwiches—they ate lots of ham at home—but filled her plate with fried chicken and a spoonful of each of the salads.

"Leave some for me!" called Jack, her next eldest brother.

Nellie saw from his plate that he was already returning for seconds.

"Pig!" she said.

While everyone ate, a brass band from Brandon played, with earth shaking tones, "Rule Brittania," "The Maple Leaf," and "God Save the Queen," as well as other songs Nellie didn't recognize. After a baseball game which pitted married men against single men, the foot races began. Nellie's fists clenched in anticipation. The winners won a nickel—enough for ice cream! She hoped there would be a foot race for girls or at least one for girls and boys together.

Her mother frowned when she mentioned it.

"Girls, racing? Certainly not. Your skirts would fly up and your legs might show."

"But the boys show their—"

"Keep silent!" said her mother.

"Keep silent!" the politician cried, looking severely at an

older Nellie where she stood at the front of the auditorium with the men. She was allowed to listen to politics but not, apparently, able to speak her mind.

Why were women only entitled to listen, staying at the back of the room like a herd of cattle? And why, when the elections came, were they not allowed to vote? Nellie pondered these questions as she listened to the rest of the politician's speech. But she didn't interrupt again. At least, not this time.

Nellie went off behind a poplar bluff and practiced keeping her skirts down as she ran among the orange lilies. It was a hard thing to do. Her dress kept wrapping itself around her legs and with the thick red drawers underneath, she felt like a tethered pony. Disgusted, she plucked at some Saskatoon berries but they weren't yet ripe and left a dusty taste in her mouth.

Soon, everyone gathered for the slow-ox race. Nellie crossed her fingers for her father's black-and-white Jake. He was a gentle little ox and so pokey that at home they harnessed him to another ox to get him going. This time though, the slowest ox of all won the prize and the prize was a big box of raisins from Read and Callendar's store.

As was the custom, owners didn't ride their own oxen. A neighbor's hired man—Jimmy Sloan—rode Jake, trying to get him to move as fast as possible by waving his straw hat and howling like a coyote. Jake, true to himself, twitched his ears and would not be hurried.

Nellie pushed Mrs. Dale's baby buggy along the hill at the side of the race, proud that Mrs. Dale was counting on her to look after baby Sara.

"Who can I count on?"

Nellie looked around at the other quilters. They were all ignoring the plea from the minister's wife to sign a petition to Parliament requesting a vote for Canadian women.

"I'll sign," Nellie said.

There were a few audible gasps from the other women. Nellie Mooney, the teacher, was going to sign the petition.

"Women should help each other," Nellie said quietly as she signed her name.

"Got a smile?" Nellie tickled baby Sara under the chin and then pushed the buggy up onto higher ground.

Suddenly, black-and-white Jake leaped forward. Jimmy Sloan was thrown sideways, sending a whisky bottle flying out of his jacket, and the ox lurched up the rise to where Nellie stood with the baby. Nellie saw him coming but she didn't run. Jake crashed past, inches away, his eyes white, his sides squeezing like a bellows. Nellie saw Jake's stomach painted with blood. Jimmy Sloan had cheated and used spurs! He got up unsteadily and started away. He was drunk.

Hot anger washed over Nellie.

"You—you—you should be *ashamed* of yourself!" she cried, the words cool on her tongue. "You should—"

"And what about you, Mrs. Nellie McClung? Who's darning your husband's socks while you're out making

your speeches?" sneered a man from the audience.

*"A woman's place is in the home, with her children!"
called another man angrily.*

"I dare say her husband's dead," muttered a woman.

*Nellie looked calmly across the hall. When she continued
speaking, her voice was pleasant.*

*"My family is well, thank you, they'll be glad you asked
after them. My husband did have a slight cold last year,
but he is quite recovered. And," she lowered her voice in a
conspiratorial whisper, "his socks are in excellent shape —
he will be delighted at your concern."*

Laughter rippled across the room.

*"But I must ask you," Nellie went on, her voice
increasing in force, "Would it be right to shut the door of
the church in the faces of half the congregation? Is is wise
to close the shop at noon, turning away half the day's
customers? Half of this town is women, am I not correct?
When you look into the eyes of your mother, your wife, your
sister...are you not ashamed to tell them that when they
travel, the only accident insurance available is for men?
Why is this? And why, when your daughters may join you
at church or at the store, are they turned away at the voters'
box?" Nellie looked into the eyes of her listeners. "Those of
you who stand in the way of half this town should be, and
I'll say it again, ashamed."*

"Ashamed!" Nellie called after Jimmy Sloan's
retreating figure.

"Hush, Nellie," said her mother, coming up the hill
to take her arm.

"No, I won't hush! He hurt our Jake and he could have hurt me. And the baby!" She stood dizzily and looked down the hill at the man who was still weaving away from the crowd.

"You should—you should—you're just a real COWARD Mr. Sloan! A REAL COWARD!" she yelled. The more she spoke, the lighter she felt, until it seemed her feet weren't touching the ground at all. "COWARD!" A white-faced Mrs. Dale gathered baby Sara in her arms, choking back sobs.

Mrs. Mooney pushed the baby buggy down the hill, leading Nellie, stiff-legged, along with it. Her mother didn't look at her when she said quietly, "You stood your ground and saved the baby, Nellie. Good girl."

"I'll stand my ground on this," said Nellie to the Premier of Manitoba.

"Take it from me, Mrs. McClung," he told her. "Nice women don't want the vote."

"Maybe your nice women aren't working in dirty factories. They're not widows begging money from their sons, and they're not watching their children go hungry while their drunken husbands do what they please," snapped Nellie. "I know many nice women in these situations and, believe me, they want to pick Members of Parliament who will make laws to help them."

The Premier didn't respond. He was thinking about what this woman was saying and wondering uncomfortably if perhaps it mightn't be better to have her on his side after all.

At the bottom of the hill, Mrs. Dale nodded at Nellie, her eyes still full of tears.

"Thank you," she said.

Nellie held her pride like a chocolate in her cheek. For once that day, she had done the right thing.

Wolves and Heathens
by Shirlee Smith-Matheson

The dogs howled in the cold still night, *Yip yip yowwl! Yip yip yowwl!* First one, then another. The sound penetrated our cabin walls and my eiderdown comforter flung over my head, but they didn't frighten me. I knew Bess's high-pitched yip, Conda's low drawn-out growl. They were sleigh dogs, working dogs, our only connection between this cabin and the string of smaller cabins which lay along the route of my father's trapline.

Dad's line lay about one hundred and fifty miles north-northwest of Fort St. John, British Columbia. It had provided us with a good living even though it meant Dad was rarely home. He logged from July to early September and trapped the rest of the year.

I was twelve in 1975, the year Dad decided to take us up on his trapline. My ten-year-old sister, Joannie, and I hugged Dad, then Mom, but Mom seemed shocked and fearful. Dad, however, was determined.

"If you and the kids come with me I won't have to close the line at Christmas," Dad went on. "We can celebrate Christmas up north, practically on Santa's doorstep!"

He winked at Joannie and me, counting on our support.

Dad sat down on a kitchen chair and ran his fingers through his hair. He looked at Mom. "Macy, I'm tired of leaving home in October, getting back for a few days at Christmas, then gone again until break-up. There will be airplanes to fly you out in an emergency and there's radio contact now, not like in the old days. I need you there...Macy."

He whispered her name, just like that, "...Macy."

It was the whisper that did it.

"All right," Mom sighed.

We had to pack efficiently, as we would be living in a two-room cabin with no store nearby. Our closest neighbour would be a trapper whose cabin was thirty miles away.

We arranged for correspondence courses, made visits to the doctor and dentist, and said goodbye to relatives. That was the hardest part.

Grandma Burton threw a fit.

"Thomas Burton, you're one crazy fool!" Grandma cried. "If you weren't my own son, I'd shoot you! Taking this poor woman and these little bits of kids up to that gawd-forsaken place."

Joannie and I stayed quiet in the other room, crossing our fingers, hoping she wouldn't wear Dad down.

Grandma paused for breath but she was far from finished. We heard her foot stomp on the floor and her voice rise. "In that wilderness country, there's nothing but wolves and heathens!"

Joannie and I burst into choking giggles barely smothered by our hands. In bed that night Joannie said in a quiet whispery voice, "What would you rather meet in the middle of the night, Sherrie? A wolf or a heathen?" On hearing the dogs burst into a sudden barking session, I said, "Hey, Joannie, do you think it's a wolf out there, or just a heathen?"

Dad hired Jimmy "Midnight" Anderson to fly us up in his old Super Cub. Jimmy was one of the best bush pilots in the North, Dad said, and he'd flown into more risky places and survived more crashes than any pilot alive.

"Any fool can fly a plane," Jimmy informed Mom, in an effort to convince her to enter the small crowded cabin, "but it takes a darned good pilot to crash 'em properly!"

I liked Jimmy Anderson. After almost every sentence, his big mouth would open in a silent laugh for about ten seconds before any sound came out. By the time it did, I was laughing my head off.

Mom wanted proof of his, and the airplane's, flying ability.

"When did you last have this plane serviced?" she asked in a small voice, after we'd left the ground.

"Oh, she had a good going-over after the last crash," Jimmy said, with a big "O" mouth.

"Have you ever been stranded after one of your, ah, crashes, with no food?" Mom asked tentatively.

"No, Ma'am," he replied. "Never had that happen. I keep a fresh coyote hanging in the back, all times, for just that kind of emergency."

Then Mom's mouth formed the "O", but a tight kind of "o." Joannie and I turned wide eyes toward the back of the airplane, about seven feet behind us. No coyote. But how could we tell, with boxes and bags of our supplies stacked to the roof? Maybe the coyote was hanging there, waiting!

Jimmy made three trips: the first with our winter provisions, and the dogsled strapped to one wing; the second with Dad, the dogs and some supplies; the third with Mom, Joannie and me and our personal belongings.

He landed on the frozen lake in front of the cabin, the long expanse of ice giving the airplane a perfect runway.

Dad had stayed when the dogs were brought in, so he had the stove going. The cabin looked small and cozy. A thin line of smoke stuck straight up from the chimney, and a thick blanket of snow draped the gable and eaves. Huge icicles, large as table legs, hung from the corners to the ground.

The dogs were tethered around the cabin, each with

a chain to its collar, looped around its separate tree. That way they could run full-circle while they weren't being used. We were told to stay outside their range and not to tease them. They were work dogs, half wild, and not pets. Only Bess, the old lead dog, could be approached. She was like a grandma to the rest, still feisty and strong, but with a more mellow temper than our grandma.

The time passed quickly through cold, flat November into colder, crisp December. Christmas was coming—Christmas!—and we couldn't do a thing. What could we buy? What could we make, with no material? Even worse, what presents could we expect way up here? Christmas would be dismal and boring.

Yip yip yip yowwl! Why couldn't they shut up? It was after ten o'clock Christmas Eve. There was nothing out there to make the dogs nervous. Wolves never came near the cabin with four Siberian Huskies tethered outside.

I lay in bed, my eyes wide, staring into the blank darkness. The smell of the wood fire in the other room blended with the pungent pine scent of the tree set up in one corner, decorated with popcorn strings and coloured paper lanterns. Beside me, Joannie slept peacefully. Mom and Dad were talking quietly in the other room. I pulled the comforter over my head, my breath warming my burrow.

Yip yip yip yowwl! Yip yip yip! Their barks seemed to increase, become faster, higher, shriller. *Yip yip yip!* I groaned and flopped over onto my stomach, burying my face into the soft pillow.

I hardly noticed the low growl until it became a steady "Burrr." Conda? A dog couldn't growl like that! "Burrrr." I lay rigid and tense so my ears would pick up every sound. Mom and Dad stopped talking. All was silent. The dogs...they were silent too!

Suddenly Dad let out a yell. "Macy, Macy, give me the lantern! Quick!"

I heard Dad shuffling into his moccasin rubbers, pictured him jabbing his arms into his moosehide jacket. I sat up in bed. What was it? "Mom! Dad!"

The "burrrr" became louder until it shook every log in the house. The dogs were going mad, howling, barking. I could hear their chains clanking as they spun around their trees.

Too frightened to move, I sat frozen in the darkness, the quilt gripped tightly to my chin. Maybe it was a mad trapper, or a Sasquatch!

"Sherrie! Joannie! Wake up. Wake up." Mom's excited cries sent shiver upon shiver up my spine. "Sherrie! Joannie!"

I punched Joannie, wildly. "Joannie, wake up! Please, wake up! We're being attacked!"

She rolled over, irritated. Stumbling and falling over the quilt, we found our way to the door. Why didn't somebody open it? The latch was stuck, the floor was cold, what was out there? Oh, Joannie! Joannie! Look! It's Santa!"

Before us stood an apparition from another world,

wearing mottled red and orange long winter underwear. Its legs were wrapped to the knees in beaded moose-hide mukluks, trimmed in long wolf fur. On its head was a red toque. Its beard was not white and flowing, but dark and stubbly. Its eyes were light blue and laughing, and there, under those eyes, right in the middle of that stubbly beard, was a big round "O".

"Merry Christmas! Merry Christmas, girls! Come and say hello to old Santa." The large mouth jumped again into its round "O" position. Throwing down a mail sack, he opened his arms. Joannie and I flew into them, crying, laughing, shrieking with joy.

To this day I'll never know how Jimmy "Midnight" Anderson found us, in the dark of night on Christmas Eve, in his little Super Cub. But I can still taste the candies and nuts and other treats he brought us, along with Christmas mail, cards and presents from our family— including Grandma Burton's big parcel.

It was a Christmas without wolves, without heathens. It was a Christmas that Joannie and I will cherish forever.

Where There's Smoke
by Constance Horne

Jim Wheatley, overcome by heat and boredom, was dozing over the accounts ledger when the office boy poked him.

"Mr. Tydeman wants to see you, Jim."

"Thanks, Denny."

Jim watched the boy head out the door. He envied him. The muggy heat would be just as bad outside, but he remembered his own days as errand boy when he often took the long way by the river road and loitered under the shade of the elm trees. As he put on his suit coat, he quickly proofread the new cheque forms that had just come from the bank.

TYDEMAN FIRE INSURANCE COMPANY
CHESTERFORD, ONTARIO
founded 1840 by Adam Tydeman

It was now 1880. Matthew Tydeman had replaced his father and continued the long tradition of service to the farmers and small town merchants of the Thames Valley in southwestern Ontario. One of their recent clients was the Pleasant Vale Cheese Company in the nearby town of Valleyfield. Earlier in the day, Jim had taken that file to Mr. Tydeman and Josh Reynolds, the investigator. The cheese factory had been completely destroyed in a nighttime fire a week ago. Because of the size of the claim, Mr. Reynolds had been sent to make sure it was legitimate. Reynolds was a hero to Jim, who dreamed of someday graduating from the boring office routine to the more exciting job of investigator.

He tapped on the door and entered the private office. Both men were in their shirtsleeves. Beads of perspiration dotted Mr. Tydeman's bald head while Josh Reynold's shirt stuck to his large body in wet patches.

· Mr. Tydeman said, "Jim, is there any reason you could not leave town for a few days?"

Jim's eyebrows rose but he answered quietly, "No, sir."

"I'm going to give you a chance to try your hand as an investigator. Mr. Reynolds is not completely satisfied with the Pleasant Vale situation."

"Nothing I can put my finger on," said the big man. "The owner, Mr. Edward Black, is a nice enough chap. Seems open and aboveboard but...."

He picked up some papers and fanned himself for a

moment. Josh Reynolds was famous in the insurance business for being able to 'smell a fraud.' Some people deliberately burned down their buildings to collect the insurance, but not many did it successfully if they were insured with Tydeman and Josh Reynolds was on the case.

"Is the claim too big?" asked Jim, trying to show an intelligent interest.

"No," answered Mr. Tydeman. "The owner is claiming $1500 for the building and $1500 for the stock of cheese he lost."

"That's about right," agreed the investigator. "I saw the report on the value of the factory and checked into the amount of milk that had been bought recently. No, it's just a feeling I have. Mr Edward Black has some debts. Lives pretty well, too. Big house. Four servants. No doubt he could use the insurance money. Trouble is, I'm known in that town now. No one's going to tell me anything."

"So, Jim, we thought we'd send you to see what you can find out," said Mr. Tydeman.

Mr. Reynolds eyed Jim doubtfully. "What's he supposed to be doing in Valleyfield?" he asked. "He's very young."

"I'm fifteen, sir."

"You can be looking for a job, then. That will give you an excuse to roam around the town and talk to people."

Valleyfield was a smaller city than Chesterford and

although the weather was just as oppressively hot, Jim enjoyed the freedom from the office and the excitement of being an investigator. After arriving on the evening train, he found a boarding house close to the station and only a block from the charred ruins of the cheese factory. He walked over to take a look. The front wall of the building was standing, but the paint had blistered and all the windowpanes were broken. The roof was completely gone. Most of it had burned and the rest had collapsed, taking down a side wall with it. Jim was about to pick his way through the rubble to see if he could find out where the fire had started when a large black dog dashed out of a stable and barked loudly. Remembering that he was not supposed to be taking a special interest in the fire, Jim retreated. Tomorrow he would start asking questions.

It was not difficult to get people to talk about the fire. The factory workers had lost their jobs. The farmers had to find other markets for their milk. Everyone agreed about the fire's bad effect on the town. But after two days Jim was discouraged. He had found out nothing new. Either he did not know the right questions to ask or the claim was legitimate.

At 5:30 on the second day, with his suit coat over his arm, he plodded up the stairs to his boarding house. A powerful stink made his nose wrinkle. The landlady pushed open the screen door for him.

"Oh, Mr. Wheatley, I'm so sorry about the smell. That stupid girl in the kitchen can't even melt a bit of cheese without burning it. She's had to throw it out and start the supper all over again."

"Is that what it is, Mrs. Perkins? Phew! Say, when the cheese factory burned the smell must have nearly knocked you out."

The woman looked at him in surprise. "Now isn't that strange? I don't remember an odour at all."

"That's impossible!"

"But it's true. I went over to watch them fighting the fire. There was just the faintest smell of burning cheese. Nothing like this." She flapped her apron to clear the air. "Isn't that strange?"

Strange? thought Jim. I'll say!

After a good supper of Welsh rarebit, he strolled over to the burned ruins. Again the black dog raced out and barked. This time, a man also came out of the stable. He was wearing overalls and thick boots and looked as old as Jim's grandfather. He called to the dog to be quiet.

"Evening," he said to Jim.

"Good evening. That's a good watch dog you have there."

The man made a face at the dog. "Think so?" he asked. "Sometimes he's too good and other times he's no good at all."

Jim laughed. "How can he be too good?"

"One night here, back a few weeks, he woke me with his barking. Before I got my pants on to see what was up, Mr. Black, the boss, looks in my door. Over at my little cottage there. 'Don't get up, Abe,' he says. 'It's just me. Checking on that new batch.' Barking at his own master! Fool dog!"

"Was that the night of the fire?"

"No, it weren't! That's what I'm telling you. It were before that. The night of the fire, the one time there's any call for the dog to bark, he don't. It was the crackling of the flames that woke me. Too late to save 'er by then." He looked sadly over the ruins. "The bucket brigade didn't even try. Just kept the stable and my cottage from going up. I give them that."

"Were there horses in the stable?"

"Aye! I got them out," said the old man proudly. "Horses, now there's an animal I love. Would you like to see them?"

Jim followed him into the stable. Two big work horses nickered to them from clean, roomy stalls.

"This here's Jack," said Abe, rubbing the animal's nose, "and that black beauty there is Emma."

"They are beautiful," said Jim, in real admiration. "What are they used for?"

"Hauling mostly. Bringing in milk from the farmers, hauling the cheeses to the railway or wherever it's going. A load of them cheese boxes can be mighty heavy. Don't faze my beauties."

"You must take great care of them."

"Not much care needed," said their groom. "They're real healthy animals." He frowned slightly. "Only once gave me any worry at all."

"Oh? What was wrong?"

The old man shrugged. "Don't know. Two weeks back both of them were very tired two mornings in a row. Like they'd been hauling all night 'stead of sleeping in their stalls. I was real scared it was sleeping sickness. Didn't last, though. Two, three days and they was fine."

Jim turned his back on Abe and petted Emma until he could control his excitement.

Casually, he asked, "When was that? Before the fire?"

"Oh, aye. Just before the fire, must have been."

Jim wanted to go back to his room and think about cheese that burned without an odor, a watch dog that didn't bark, and horses that were tired in the morning. But Abe wanted to talk. He was worried about losing his job. If the factory wasn't rebuilt, there would be no need of a watchman. They went outside and sat on two empty round cheese boxes labeled *Rogers Box Co. of Toronto*. The dog stretched out at the old man's feet.

Later, lying on his bed, kept awake by the heat and his own excitement, Jim thought about the boxes. Josh Reynolds had questioned the factory employees and they all said they had seen boxes of cheese stored in the cool room. Since there was no smell of burning cheese, the boxes must have been empty. Where were the full ones? Jim had checked and none had been shipped from the Valleyfield station for two months. So, there were two things he must do in the morning. Having decided that, Jim slept.

Next day, the first thing he did was send a ten-word telegram to Josh Reynolds: *Did* Rogers Box Co.

Toronto *sell extra boxes our client. Stop.*

Then he boarded the train and rode up the line to the next station. To get the station master's cooperation, he had to show his letter from Mr. Tydeman. The freight office waybills showed that in the week before the fire two shipments of cheese, equalling about half of what was supposed to have burned, had been shipped from this station.

"I remember that," said the station master. "I came down one morning and found all these boxes of cheese and a man waiting to ship it. He helped me load it on the train when she came in."

The description of the man did not fit Mr. Black. But that doesn't matter, thought Jim. He must have had an accomplice. He couldn't lift those boxes by himself. Probably, while the other man stayed with the shipment, Mr. Black drove his horses back to their stable.

When the east-bound train came in, Jim boarded and rode past Valleyfield to the next station. There he found the same thing. Cheese had been shipped from there before the fire. Waiting for the afternoon train was agony. At last, hot and sticky, covered with cinders and soot, he went into the Valleyfield Station and collected his telegram. *Yes double order boxes shipped July 25. Stop.*

Grinning broadly, Jim almost ran back to the boarding house. He washed up, ate a good supper and then hurried to Mr. Black's large brick home. When he said he was from the Tydeman Insurance Company, he was taken immediately into the owner's study where he was greeted politely by a pleasant looking middle-aged man.

"Excuse my shirtsleeves, won't you? This heat is terrible. Take off your coat, if you like."

"No, I won't, thanks."

"Well, sit down," said Mr. Black as he seated himself behind the desk. "You've brought my cheque, I suppose."

"No, Mr. Black, I haven't. I've been investigating your claim on behalf of the company."

"But that's been done by Mr. Reynolds. "

"He wasn't quite satisfied," said Jim quietly.

"You found nothing irregular," said Mr. Black.

"Yes, I did, sir. I know the cheese was all shipped out secretly before the fire and empty boxes substituted for full ones."

Color drained from the man's cheeks.

Jim went on, "I suspect you set that fire yourself. That's why the dog didn't bark. You and an accomplice had been at the plant at least two different nights. The dog was accustomed to your being there, but one night he barked at your accomplice. You took the dog with you after you started the fire not to raise the alarm."

Mr. Black stood up. "You'd better leave my house," he said coldly.

"I will," answered Jim. "Tomorrow I'm going back to Chesterford to make my report.

"Case closed, as Mr. Reynolds would say," he murmured to himself.

Shadows of the Past
by John Wilson

It was a wet afternoon and I was bored. That was the trouble with holidays at the old cottage on Mayne Island—when it rained there was nothing to do.

My name is Sarah and most summers Mom and I come over from Vancouver for a few weeks. Usually Dad stays behind to work and joins us on weekends. The cabin is really old. Mom says it was one of the first houses on the island and was built by her great grandmother, Emily. None of the walls are quite straight.

The cottage is a great place when the sun is shining; there are beaches, boats and walks in the woods. But on the afternoon I found the letter it was raining. There's no TV and I had read all the books I had brought with me and I'd had it up to here with Clue and Monopoly. I was hanging around the kitchen and I guess I looked bored.

"Why don't you go and look through the books in

the front room," Mom suggested. "Maybe you'll find something to read there."

"They're all boring and old."

"Yes, some of them are," Mom replied, "but there are a couple of interesting books on local history."

"History's boring too. It's just about a bunch of dead people and what they did a long time ago."

"Sarah," Mom said firmly, "I'm going to make supper and I can't do it with you moping around and getting under my feet all the time."

Reluctantly I shuffled into the other room. Outside the rain was still lashing down. The clouds looked heavy and black and seemed to cast a dark shadow over the whole island. My gaze drifted over to the bookcase. It didn't look promising. Three narrow shelves of dull brown spines; some of the books must be a hundred years old. Probably written in Latin, by monks. Still, I pulled one out. It had that "old book" smell, and the spine cracked as I opened it. It was called *Narratives of the Gulf Islands* and was printed in 1954. That made it the same age as Mom.

I knew "narratives" were stories, so I began to thumb through it looking for something interesting. That something fell out onto the floor at my feet. It was three sheets of folded, yellowed paper—a letter.

Usually I don't read other people's letters, but this one was dated, September 13th, 1933, so I figured no one would mind now. It was addressed to Sadie. I guessed that must be my Grandma Sadie who lives down in Surrey now. She would have been twelve, my age exactly, in 1933. The letter was signed Grandma Emily Park, so she must have been my great great grandmother, the Emily who built this cabin. This is what the letter said:

"Dearest Sadie, things are very quiet here since you and your mother moved to Vancouver. It was nice of you to write and ask me to come and live with you, but I'm sixty-eight—seems awful old doesn't it?—and I've lived all my life on this island. Everything I see out of my window is familiar and brings to mind a story. It's as if I am surrounded by the shadows of my past and I think I would miss them terribly if I left. So I thank you for your kind offer, dear, but I have to say no. I do hope you understand. Perhaps it would help if I told you some of the things I remember, then maybe you might see what I would be leaving.

"I remember some important things, like poor little Margaret dying of the pneumonia in the hard snowy winter of '96, and I remember some funny things like the time the old cow jumped out of the rowboat and swam clear across Active Pass. I even remember some strange things such as how much the Victoria Chinese paid for deer skins and that a gallon of dogfish livers could fetch 25¢ from the loggers over at New Westminster. They used to use the oil from the livers and some used to eat them raw, can you imagine that? Said the vitamins kept them healthy! We didn't mind what they did with them, the money for them was what kept us alive in the early days.

"My father was one of the first settlers on Mayne. He was an island man from Shetland in the cold ocean north of Scotland. It's a place with no trees and I can still see him as an old man standing looking at the giant firs and cedars on this island and just shaking his head in wonder. He was a big man, but he had such a soft voice, especially when he used to sing me lullabies in the soft, lilting tongue of his native land.

"He ran away from home at fourteen for the lure of three meals a day on board ship. That was in 1849. There was the potato famine and my father had a brother or sister for every year of his age around the dinner table. Like so many others, he jumped ship in Victoria and headed for the Cariboo goldfields around Barkerville in the interior. Also like most of the others he never found any gold, although he made a good living running a stopping house. That's where he met my mother. She was a Lillooet woman and he brought her down to the island with him in 1863, just two years before I was born. They never had a paper marriage, but a lot of folks never bothered with the formality in those days.

"Most of the time life was easy, at least for the children. In the woods we caught fat grouse to sell to the steamer passengers in the Pass. The old *Princess Louise* used to come through at night, all lit up like a floating palace, and those that wanted to catch her had to row out and climb on board.

"We used to row everywhere—over to Galiano or down to Pender—and my brothers took us out fishing in the rowboat. One time your great uncle Will went out on his own and got swept out of the Pass by the tide and didn't get back till the next day, all wet and cold and sorry for himself. After that, we couldn't go out unless someone older came with us.

"There was no school to go to in those days. It only started in 1883 when Mrs. Monk taught a class of thirty children from all the nearby islands. But that was too late for me. I was eighteen by then and had a husband and the first of five babies.

"I married Charlie when I was sixteen. It wasn't an arranged marriage, but I didn't have a lot of say about it either. It just seemed that everyone thought it was a good idea and, eventually, Charlie and I did too.

"We started out by raising sheep and selling lambs. By the second year we had saved enough money to buy a cow. Not that we made a lot of money farming in those days. Charlie always had to go fishing or building to make ends meet, but we managed and the children always had warm clothes and enough food. In fact, in a good year we were quite well off. One year Charlie and his partners caught nearly seven thousand salmon in the Fraser River run and sold them for four cents each. The money that year bought us lumber for a barn.

"Spring was the busiest time. There was the planting to be done and the lambing. We used to let the sheep range free over the whole north end of the island with only a tar mark on their coats to say whose they were, so at lambing time everyone went out to bring in their own in so we could protect the sheep and new lambs from the cougars. After a hard winter, the cougars would have no fear and would come right down into the farm looking for something to eat.

"I remember one day, it would have been in the spring of '84—your mother, Becky, was only two and was playing out in the dirt behind the house with the rag doll I had sewn for her that winter. I was in the house sweeping the floor. I don't know why, maybe a movement caught my eye, but I looked out the kitchen window. It was sunny but there was a deep shadow over in the corner under the apple tree. I had to look twice to be sure, but crouching in the shadow watching Becky there was an old skinny cougar.

"I didn't think. I screamed, and kept on screaming as I ran out the door waving the broom around my head. I must have looked like I had gone mad, because I scared your Mom, but I scared that old cougar too and he ran off into the bush. I grabbed Becky and the pair of us just sat in the dirt in tears until we calmed down. After that, Charlie always left a gun beside the door, but I used to tease him that a frightened mother with a broom was more than a match for any man with a gun.

"In the summer we were always busy picking the apples and pears to be sent to the market in Victoria. The soil on the island was good and there was plenty of fertilizer from the plowing oxen or the horses. There was a small creek that ran down to the bay, but some years it dried up completely. Then we would have to use rainwater from the storage barrels. First we would take some to drink, then the clothes got washed, then the kids, then the floors and lastly the dog. What water was left was pretty black by the time we threw it on the vegetables.

"Once we got established, we hired occasional help with the work. One year we hired a Chinaman called Lee. He was a small, wiry man who always wore traditional clothes and his hair in a ponytail down the back. He seemed nice enough and he worked hard, but he and his family were running an illegal rice whisky still. Of course he was caught; my island has always been too small to keep a big secret. He was given a three year jail sentence. When they took him away, he left a tin of his money on a shelf behind the back door. The following year I heard a noise in the kitchen in the middle of the night and got up to see what it was. There was a full moon which lit up the yard and the back door was open.

"There stood Lee with the tin in his hand. 'Thank you misses,' he said and darted out the door into the night.

"I was confused, he should have been in prison in Victoria, not skulking around in my kitchen. It was only after he was released that I heard the story. Lee was smart. He knew that, to most white people, all Chinese looked alike. He was allowed a visitor every two weeks and he asked for his cousin who was about the same height and build as himself. When the cousin arrived, they changed clothes and Lee walked free for two weeks. The guards never looked too closely. They were happy as long as one Chinaman went in and only one came out.

"One fall Charlie planted a small orchard so we had fruit; apples and plums mostly although we did try peaches. Fall was also the time that my island was called "Little Hell." We had a saloon over at the old Point Comfort Hotel and some of the people on the surrounding islands were on the temperance side—you know, against the evils of liquor. Of course, that didn't stop some of them rowing over to examine the place more closely from time to time.

"The only trouble we had was with the miners who were working claims up in the Cariboo and came down here to spend their winters. Sometimes their parties got a little out of hand and a couple of them would spend a night in the lockup to cool off, but mostly it was just good-natured fun. The boys knew that if they did over-step the bounds too much they would have Canon Paddon to answer too. The Canon wouldn't stand any nonsense, either from his seven sons or from his flock of parishioners. He had been one of the few lucky ones to survive when the streetcar went off the Point Ellice bridge into Victoria's Gorge in '96. All he suffered was shock and a few bruises. I'll always remember him telling us that being resuscitated after the fall into the river was a much worse sensation than drowning.

"When he died, in 1922, he was almost eighty. He instructed that his burial service be conducted at five in the morning. That way, only the parishioners who loved him would make the effort to attend. We all did, as did some of the miners he used to threaten with the fire and brimstone.

"Well now Sadie, its almost winter, and I think I'll stay and see it through. I don't know what I would do if I couldn't look out the window at the tree where the cougar stood or keep my knick-knacks on the shelf where old Lee's tin sat. My past is all around me, so you see, I cannot leave it behind. You're only twelve and you've still got a past to make, but one day you'll understand.

"Anyway, I hope you are making many good friends in Vancouver. Maybe you will come over and visit me in the spring.

Much love,
Grandma Emily Park

I finished reading just as Mom shouted, "Supper's ready, Sarah."

I folded the letter, put it back in the book, and went out to the kitchen. I looked, and there was Lee's shelf behind the back door. I stood and stared out the window. The rain had stopped and the yard was bright with sunlight. In the far corner was an old, gnarled apple tree. It cast a deep, irregular shadow on the ground. I had to look twice, sure I'd seen a tawny shape crouched there in the dark.

Remember, Chrysanthemum

by Kathryn Hatashita-Lee

In the school hallways, the kids call her "Speedbump" Woodley due to a rollerblading accident that summer when she had broken her arm, but her real name is Allison Kiku Woodley, an identity that hints at her dual heritage. Her father is of English descent and reads about samurai swords; her mother is of Japanese descent and studies Victorian literature. *Kiku* is Japanese for chrysanthemum, a flower that blooms for many days and graces pottery and kimono fabrics.

When Allison leaves her home near Vancouver's English Bay and skates across town to visit her Grandmother Tanaka, she is met by a white ceramic cat with one raised paw. The cat is a *maneki neko,* or a beckoning cat, bringing good fortune to homes and businesses.

On bookshelves, and on the television stand are

many albums of family photos. Every photo on their pages is held in place with silver corners. Allison liked leafing through their pages: her grandmother as a girl and a young woman; the giant trees of Lynn Valley, where the family often picnicked on a sushi lunch....

Allison thought she had seen every album in the collection, but one day Grandma Tanaka pulled out a black case tucked under some old hat boxes. Allison quietly opened the latches and pulled back the top. Inside were piled more black and white photos waiting for her fingers to sift through their filmy images.

"Take your time, Allison Kiku," said her grandmother.

Allison spread the photos on the floor and let the blue carpet disappear beneath the white borders of the prints. "Is that you and Great-Grandma and Great-Grandpa?" she asked.

"Yes. You can see my seven brothers and sisters all lined up. Your great-grandmother is holding my brother, Tosh. He was just a baby," said Allison's grandmother. "The old frame house still stands in East Vancouver."

Allison picked up a photo of a class with rows of students holding long needles from which dangled partially completed pieces of knitting. Almost all the students looked Japanese.

"My grade six teacher at Lord Strathcona Elementary took that photo in January 1942," Mrs. Tanaka began. "During the War, World War II, I mean, our whole class knitted sweaters to clothe the British schoolchildren. The girl beside me knitted one sleeve, and I knitted the other one. My sleeve came out a couple inches shorter. I still feel sorry for the British schoolgirl who received our lopsided gift."

"Mom says your whole family left Vancouver by train that spring," said Allison. "You lost your home and all your things and went to a sort of prison."

"Yes. That was during the evacuation. Japan had bombed Pearl Harbor in Hawaii in December 1941. William Lyon Mackenzie King was Prime Minister of Canada at that time, and he decided we were a threat, so he ordered us out. Our Uncle Kenji's fishing boat was impounded, taken away from him and sold to strangers, at Annieville Dyke on the Fraser River. We were Vancouver-born children of a landscape gardener; we were Canadians, but to the government, we were 'enemies.' I still have your great-grandmother's picture i.d. labelled *enemy alien*."

"That's no thanks for all those sweaters you knit for the war effort!" said Allison. Her grandmother's face clouded over and her jaw tightened slightly.

Allison looked over the collection and pointed to another yellowed photo of a family wearing overalls and sitting on a wagon. "We were sent to a sugar beet farm in southern Alberta. Harvesting was backbreaking work, but no Caucasians wanted that kind of work. We had no electricity or running water. We did our home-work by the light of a coal-oil lamp. My sisters used a bucket to draw water out of a cistern. When we cooked rice, the water turned the rice yellowish-green," Allison's grandmother continued.

Allison pointed to a photo of a lady with a cow and a bucket. "Your Great-Aunt Miyoko always milked Bossy the cow. After the war, our family moved to a big city in Ontario and never lived in the country again," said Mrs. Tanaka.

The last photo in the pile was of a parade float with a row of Japanese Canadian girls, all clad in kimonos, aboard its long platform.

"I took that photo in 1956, during the Dominion Day parade in Toronto. Do you see my friend, Keiko, second to the left? The Japanese Canadian Citizens' Association organized that float. Everyone in the crowd applauded," she said nostalgically.

"I don't think I could stand being in a kimono or having my hair pulled up like that," said Allison.

Her grandmother chuckled and said gently, "You shouldn't feel embarrassed about the way you look, especially if you're wearing our ancestors' clothing. Try a kimono sometime. You might like it."

"Maybe," said Allison doubtfully. "Thank you for telling your stories, Grandma." As Allison Kiku headed for the door, she winked at the white cat.

"Think of a museum as a gathering place where yesterday meets today," said Mrs. Epstein to her class. Allison and her classmates stood near the giant stainless steel crab outside the Vancouver Museum and Pacific

Space Centre. Inside the gift shop, Allison saw a Japanese tourist pull out a crisp fifty-dollar bill with the reddish-orange image of Mackenzie King on one side, and a snowy owl on the other. She remembered her grandmother's story and felt haunted by the late Prime Minister's gaze as the class walked to the exhibit.

Under the red and white banners hanging from the ceiling, the class wandered around the display of Japanese samurai sword guards in the *Soul of the Samurai* exhibit. Allison peered closely at the small round sword guards she thought looked like large iron coins with holes. When attached to a sword, the sword guard or *tsuba,* prevented the warrior's hand from slipping onto the sharp blade.

Most of the sword guards showed flowers, birds, and insects carved in low relief. Allison saw dark dragons lurking in clouds or waves. Although dragons are popular in the supernatural world, Allison felt uneasy when the display's description said seeing an entire dragon's body meant death.

Another display case showed the work of eighteenth-century artisan, Nagatsune, who applied an inlay of brass, as well as silver and gold, or an overlay of high-relief carvings to create a colourful picture. Allison really liked the scene of three graceful silver herons and golden plants highlighted against the dark ironwork background of the sword guard.

Mrs. Epstein turned to her and said, "I know you were born here, Allison, but have you been to Japan?"

"No," replied Allison. She remembered her Aunt Grace saying at the family reunion in Ontario last year, "Japan's the last place I'd want to visit."

Allison pulled herself out of her recollections and focused on what was in front of her. The large mural of a fierce Samurai warrior looked very foreign to Allison.

"Do you speak Japanese at home, Allison?" asked Mrs. Epstein.

"No," Allison replied again. She remembered her Great-Uncle Tosh and his memories of the Japanese Language School on Alexander Street: "Every day after school I took the streetcar to Japanese School. That made for a really long day. When the Japanese School closed after Pearl Harbor, I was so glad. No more lessons in Japanese!"

"Do you eat Japanese food at home, Allison?" asked her classmate, Tasha.

"No," replied Allison. She was getting tired of all these questions. She remembered sitting on her bed, unwrapping a small parcel of fruitcake Grandma Tanaka sent, not from Japan, but from Marks & Spencer!

"Hey, Allison," whispered her classmate, Vladimir. "Did you know you're part Japanese?"

"Stop bugging her," said Yvonne. "Allison is just like us. She always gets the top marks in English."

I wonder what was really on exhibit, the samurai sword guards or me? Allison wondered as they headed for the exit.

Later that spring Grandma Tanaka died. Allison returned to her house for the last time.

"I'm surprised Grandma told you as much as she did about those photos," said Allison's mother.

"Maybe she knew she had to tell somebody," said Allison.

"Your grandparents and great-grandparents didn't like to talk about the evacuation. I remember your Great-Uncle Tosh shrugging and saying, 'It can't be helped.'"

Allison looked sadly around the living room full of old albums.

Her mother was looking through Grandma Tanaka's papers when she found a heavy cream-coloured paper with Canada's coat of arms. In both English and French, the words of then Prime Minister Brian Mulroney acknowledged:

...the Government of Canada, on behalf of all Canadians, does hereby: 1) acknowledge that the treatment of Japanese Canadians during and after World War II was unjust and violated principles of human rights as they are understood today; 2) pledge to ensure, to the full extent that its powers allow, that such events will not happen again; and 3) recognize, with great respect, the fortitude and determination of Japanese Canadians who, despite great stress and hardship, retain their commitment and loyalty to Canada and contribute so richly to the development of the Canadian nation."

Allison's father arranged for the Grandma Tanaka's

furniture to be donated to a senior citizens' lodge. Allison was told to choose a small memento of her grandmother for herself.

Allison pulled out the handle of the black case with latches. She filed through the aged photographs looking for the five photos she knew. She looked up, half expecting to see her grandmother sitting at her side.

Allison carefully placed the photos in an old envelope she found postmarked 1942. She took off her square neck scarf and wrapped the envelope in a neat bundle inside her knapsack. Allison also packed away the white ceramic cat.

As she turned her back to leave for the last time you could just see two eyes peeking out under the canvas flap and one slender paw beckoning good luck.

One Candle, Many Lights
by Kathleen Cook Waldron

For a small town, Lone Butte celebrated Christmas in a big way. The moment calendars were flipped from November to December, green garlands, silver tinsel, and decorations of every description seemed to sprout and bloom on houses, stores, and streetlights. In the window of Eaton's catalogue store, a star of Bethlehem appeared on the rabbit ears of the only television in town. Clerks from Hank's Feed and Coal Store to Pearl's Ready-to-Wear dragged out record players and sent conflicting choruses of Christmas carols drifting down Main Street. "Frosty the Snowman" and Bing Crosby's "White Christmas" could be heard wrapping themselves around scratchy LPs, their notes dancing on the winter wind like snowflakes.

Before David was old enough to go to school, he thought the cheery decorations and music were just Lone Butte's way of making winter seem warmer. It wasn't until he started school that David discovered *Christmas.*

At first he accepted Christmas as simply one more thing he was expected to do in school, like spelling or math. He helped bake Christmas cookies, and he sang Christmas songs, even though he had no idea what "In Excelsius Deo" meant or what a "manger" was. While his classmates competed for starring roles as kings, wisemen, or angels in the Christmas programs, David preferred to be a donkey, a lamb, or a camel.

David thought he knew all he needed to know about Christmas. Until now.

Just before the final bell rang to go home, his teacher, Miss Wagner, made an announcement, "I have something very special for all of you to do tonight: I want you to think about your favorite Christmas!"

"I know mine!" Dennis shouted. "We had a ham that was bigger than my baby brother."

"I got a Purple People Eater hula hoop!" Nancy added.

"My whole family went riding in a one horse open sleigh. Hey!" Jimmy yelled, shaking a pair of invisible reins.

"Good," Miss Wagner replied. "Tonight I want all of you to think about what happened on your favorite Christmas. Tomorrow you'll start writing. And next week you'll all have a chance to read your stories out loud."

The bell rang and David burst out the door. Dennis' mom offered him a ride in her new Edsel, but David flew by without noticing. He ran all the way home.

The moment he opened the door, David forgot about Christmas. The warm smell of potato pancakes greeted him. *Latkes!* Two skillets sizzled on the stove as his mother spooned fresh batter into the hot oil.

David's younger twin sisters, Sarah and Susan, were busy preparing *latke* toppings. Sarah poured cold applesauce into a glass bowl. Susan scooped sour cream into another. David reached for his favorite topping: ketchup.

"Happy Hanukkah!" their dad called as he walked in the door. Susan, Sarah, and David smothered him with hugs. "Happy Hanukkah!" they all yelled.

With a final polish, Mom placed their *menorah*, the nine-cupped Hanukkah candleholder, on the window sill beside a small box of colorful, spiral candles. At sunset, Dad lit the *shammos*, the helper candle, and with it he lit one candle in the *menorah* for the first night of Hannukkah. When he placed the *shammos* back in the *menorah*, everyone sang the blessing.

As always on the first night, Dad told the story of Hanukkah.

"Over two thousand years ago, Alexander the Great conquered western Asia and northern Africa. Most of the people he conquered adopted his Greek ways. Only in Judea, one of the smallest states in Alexander's powerful empire, did people continue to live as their fathers had.

"For over a hundred years," Dad explained, "the Judeans survived in relative peace. Then Antiochus Epiphanes took over the throne of Syria, Judea's neighbour to the north. Antiochus decreed that all of his subjects had to follow Greek ways. He took over the Judeans' Temple and ordered them to to worship Zeus. When the Judeans refused, Antiochus vowed to destroy them. One brave man, Mattathias, with his five sons led the Judeans in a revolt. When Mattathias died, his son, Judah Maccabee, continued to lead his few untrained soldiers against hundreds of Syrian mercenaries. After three years of fighting, Judah and his followers, known as the Maccabees, defeated their enemies and took back the Temple.

"After they reclaimed the Temple," Dad concluded, "the Judeans wanted to relight its holy *menorah*, but they could only find only a small jugful of oil, enough to burn for only one night. But those few drops of oil burned until more could be found: eight days and nights. A great miracle happened there!"

"A miracle!" David and his sisters agreed. Dad reached in his pocket for the children's Hanukkah coins, their *gelt*. As always, the first night's *gelt* was two shiny pennies. Susan and Sarah put theirs in their loafers, but David put his in his bank. Before sitting down to dinner, everyone sang "Ma'oz Tsur," "Rock of Ages," in Hebrew and in English.

At school the next morning Miss Wagner took out her guitar and everyone sang "Oh Christmas Tree" in

English and German and "Silent Night" in English and French.

After Miss Wagner put away her guitar, she handed out sheets of paper. "You've all had a chance to think about your favorite Christmas," she said. "Now let's start writing."

Everyone started writing. Except David. David simply sat. He watched Dennis' pencil fly across the page. He watched Jimmy draw a tree. But David didn't even pick up his pencil.

"Are you all right, David?" Miss Wagner asked, "Do you need any help?"

"Yes. Er, I mean no, Miss Wagner. I don't need any help."

David started to scribble. Not a single word made sense, but he knew that as long as he looked busy Miss Wagner would leave him alone. When the bell rang, David crumpled his paper and threw it away.

At home Susan counted almonds evenly into five small bowls. "One for Dad, one for Mom, one for David, one for Sarah, and one for ME!" she said as she divided up the almonds. While Susan got the almonds ready for placing bets on tonight's *dreydel* game, Sarah sat on the kitchen floor practicing by spinning a *dreydel* over and over. David watched her spin the small, four-sided top. Each time it fell, a different Hebrew letter showed: N(un), G(imel), H(ey), or S(hin) representing the words *Nes Gadol Hayah Sham,* meaning "A great miracle happened there."

With each spin, Sarah sang, *"Nun* means that I get none, *Shin* means I put one in, *Hey* means that I get half, but *Gimel* means I win 'em all!"

At sunset, Dad lit the *shammos* and gave it to Susan to light two candles for the second night of Hanukkah. She chose her favorite Hanukkah song: *"Oh, dreydel, dreydel, dreydel. I made it out of clay, and when it's dry and ready, then dreydel I shall play!"* Everyone sang, although David thought they might sound better with Miss Wagner's guitar. The second night's *gelt* was a nickel. David didn't know what his sisters planned to do with theirs, but he could already taste the chocolate bar he would buy with his at Olsen's store.

After dinner, the *dreydel* game began. Everyone placed an almond in the center of the table. Sarah spun first. "Look!" she shouted. *"Gimel!* I win!"

"That's *Nun,"* David corrected. *"Nun* means you get nothing."

Sarah shrugged, "I'll win next time," she promised. But in the end, David won by six almonds.

The next morning Miss Wagner filled two dozen big bowls with popcorn and cranberries. Most of the morning was spent nibbling and giggling while everyone strung soft puffs of popcorn to tart, juicy berries. At noon, Jimmy's dad brought in a big fir tree. Everyone sang *"Deck the halls with boughs of holly!"* as they laced long red and white strings through the tree's soft green needles.

"Do you have your Christmas tree yet?" Jimmy

asked between verses.

"No," David replied. Why tell him that not only did he not have *this* year's tree, he *never* had a tree.

"We have ours," Dennis told them, "and it's so tall my mom says its top tickles the ceiling."

"Fa, la, la, la, la, la, la, la, la!" Jimmy and David replied.

When writing time came again, David's classmates took out yesterday's pages and went to work. David took a clean sheet of paper from Miss Wagner's desk and sat down.

Chewing on the end of his pencil, he stared at the paper. He could hear Miss Wagner making her rounds. He had to start writing.

"My favorite Christmas," he began, covering his paper with his elbows.

Miss Wagner walked by and David leaned over his page, *"My favorite Christmas was...."*

What? David wondered. What can I say?

"My favorite Christmas," David wrote, *"was with Uncle Morris and Auntie Zel. Last Christmas they brought us a 500 foot tall Christmas tree. It was so tall we had to cut a hole in our roof. It took ten tons of popcorn and fifty million cranberries to decorate it."*

On the third night of Hanukkah, David and his sisters cut out paper *menorahs* and *dreydels*. Standing on chairs, they taped their paper cutouts to the walls and hung them with strings from the ceiling.

"I hope you're not ticklish," David said to the ceiling

as he stuck it with tape.

"What's that?" Mom asked.

"Nothing," David said, giving the tape an extra thump with his fist.

At sunset, Sarah lit three candles and chose to sing: *"On this night, let us light three little shining candles. 'Tis a sight, oh so bright, three little shining candles."*

For the third night's *gelt,* David and his sisters each got a dime. David's dime, along with the *gelt* from the nights to come, would go into his bank. He was saving for a Brownie camera, like the one in the Eaton's catalogue picture he had taped to his door.

Thursday morning when the time came to take out their stories, Ricky said, "I can't decide if I want Santa to bring me Rocket Richard hockey skates or a Robin Roberts baseball glove."

"I'm asking for blue suede shoes," Nancy said, doing her best Elvis imitation. "And don't you...step on my blue suede shoes!"

"What would *you* do with blue suede shoes?" Ricky asked. "You're a girl."

"So?"

A sharp look from Miss Wagner ended the discussion.

Jimmy whispered to David, "I'm asking Santa for a genuine Davy Crockett 'coonskin cap. What are you asking for?"

David pretended not to hear. He took out his paper and wrote, *"Our Christmas tree was so tall that when Santa came, his reindeer fell through the hole in the roof.*

Piles of presents scattered everywhere, and we all had a groovy time singing, dancing, and opening packages."

At home Sarah and Susan were coloring a "Happy Hanukkah" banner on the kitchen table.

"Want to help?" Susan asked.

"Here's a good blue," Sarah said, offering him the biggest crayon she could find.

"No, thanks," David sighed. "I've done enough writing today."

At sunset David lit four candles and led his favorite Hanukkah song: *"Who can retell the things that befell us? Who can count them? In every age a hero or sage came to our aid."*

David dropped his *gelt,* a quarter, into his bank. He gave the bank a long hard shake, then slammed it down on his desk.

Everyone at school celebrates Christmas, he thought. No one celebrates Hanukkah, except us. Why do we have to be different?

On Friday David finished his story: *"I hope Uncle Morris and Auntie Zel bring us tons of presents and an even bigger tree this year."*

Miss Wagner had the class put away their stories. "Monday we'll practice for our Christmas play, but I'll be looking forward to hearing your stories on Tuesday," she said.

As soon as the bell rang, David ran out the door, forgetting about Christmas and his story.

At home Mom, Sarah, and Susan were busy making

latkes. Dad had come home early and was waiting for him. "Let's go, David," he said. "The train arrives at three thirty." The Studebaker was still warm when Dad and David climbed inside. Dad started the engine and David felt the thrill of it rush through him. Dad only used the car for work and special occasions. And this was definitely a special occasion.

They pulled out of their bumpy driveway, turned, and headed across town to the train station. Traffic moved slowly as cars and holiday shoppers crowded Lone Butte's single paved street. Dad and David both waved to people they knew. The engine idled noisily as they waited for Mrs. Higgins to make a left turn in front of them. While they were waiting, Jimmy walked by with his mother. He stopped and knocked on David's window.

"Are you coming tonight?" Jimmy asked.

"What?" David asked, rolling down his window.

"At six o'clock all the town Christmas lights will be turned on at once! Hundreds of them! And...."

But before Jimmy could finish, Mrs. Higgins made her turn.

"There'll be cookies and hot chocolate for everyone," Jimmy shouted at the moving car. David waved and rolled up his window.

They got to the station just as the train was pulling in. David could see Uncle Morris, Auntie Zel, and his cousins, Danny and Judy, standing inside. For a fraction of a second, David's Christmas story flashed across his mind. Where's the tree, he wondered? Then he caught himself. Uncle Morris and Auntie Zel had missed a day of work and let Danny and Judy miss a day of school so they could come all the way from Vancouver to celebrate Hanukkah with their family. They would not be bringing a Christmas tree. Ever.

As soon as Uncle Morris and Auntie Zel stepped off the train, David was caught up in a flurry of hugs, kisses, and exclamations of "How you've grown!". He barely had time to say hello to Danny and Judy before Dad had the car loaded with shopping bags, suitcases, Auntie, Uncle, and cousins. In the front seat, Dad chatted happily with Uncle Morris and Auntie Zel while David and his cousins whispered and giggled in the back.

Driving back through town was even slower than coming in. As they waited for cars and holiday shoppers, several of David's classmates waved and called, "See you tonight!"

"What's happening tonight?" Uncle Morris asked, turning to David in the back seat.

"They're lighting the holiday lights in town," David told him. "Hundreds of them." Then trying to sound casual, he added, "Maybe we could go?"

Uncle Morris looked blank. David already knew how his parents felt about Christmas celebrations. "We're Jewish," they always told him. "Our traditions are different. Celebrate and be proud of who we are." But David wasn't proud. He didn't want to be different. Maybe Uncle Morris would understand.

"Everyone in Lone Butte celebrates Christmas, Uncle Morris. Everyone! The whole town. They have Christmas trees and Santa Claus, Christmas dinners and Christmas carols. Cookies and pageants and lights. Everything!"

For a few moments only the sound of the engine could be heard in the car.

Then Uncle Morris said, "No one else celebrates Hanukkah here?"

"No one," David replied firmly.

"So," Uncle Morris said slowly, "if I understand correctly, everyone in Lone Butte celebrates Christmas, except for us."

"Right, Uncle Morris. Everyone."

"So, if we don't celebrate Hanukkah, who will?"

David had no answer.

As soon as the Studebaker pulled into the driveway, Sarah and Susan ran outside with their Hanukkah banner to welcome the new arrivals. Their mother held open the front door, surrounded by the sweet scents of brisket, *latkes*, and warm chocolate cake.

Before David's dad stepped inside, he raised his suitcase and pointed to the rosy glow on the hills, "The sun's about to set," he said, "and we have candles to light."

First Uncle Morris lit the candles for the fifth night of Hanukkah. After the blessing he said, "Now the Sabbath candles." Like Hanukkah and all Jewish holidays, the Sabbath started at sunset, but because no work was permitted on the Sabbath, not even lighting a fire, the Sabbath candles had to be lit after the Hanukkah candles. According to tradition, the 'ladies' of the house lit the Sabbath candles and sang the blessing. Once all the candles were lit, Dad gave each of the five children a fifty cent piece.

"I have something special for the children, too," Uncle Morris said, reaching into a shopping bag. As he pulled out his hand, David saw one of the numbers tatooed on his uncle's forearm. Both Uncle Morris and Auntie Zel had those numbers. Frightening words echoed through David's mind as he remembered when Uncle Morris had first told him about the numbers and the Nazis' terrible answer to what they called "the Jewish question."

"Sometimes simply surviving can be a great victory," Uncle Morris had concluded. David shivered.

"Are you with us, David?" Uncle Morris asked, handing him a big bag of chocolate *gelt*. "Or don't you like these?"

David smiled, thanked his uncle, and ripped open the netted bag of dark chocolate coins wrapped in gold foil. He had three chocolates stuffed in his mouth before anyone else could peel the foil off a single coin.

The weekend flew by. David and Danny spent the days sledding and playing hockey. Susan, Sarah, and Judy, their pony-tails flying, bopped in their bobby socks and poodle skirts to Bobby Darin and Paul Anka. Once, coming inside to warm up, the boys found the girls miming swimming strokes in rhythm to the music.

"I'm Marilyn Bell," Sarah said, "Canada's sweetheart!"

In unison, Susan and Judy pretended to dive. "Here we go," Judy said, "across the icy waters of Lake Ontario and across the English Channel!"

"Large charge," Danny said. "You've been Marilyn Bell now for four years. Can't you think of anything else?" Before anyone could answer, Danny did his best imitation of a cannonball jump into the middle of the girls' dance floor, while David splashed them madly with invisible water.

On the sixth and seventh nights of Hanukkah, first Danny, then Judy lit the candles. The *gelt* both nights was a shiny silver dollar! By the time Uncle Morris and Auntie Zel left on Sunday, David's pockets bulged with almonds, and his belly bulged with *latkes*.

On Monday David was too busy with play practice to think about his story. But before the final bell rang, Miss Wagner reminded everyone, "Tomorrow we'll hear your Christmas stories," she said. "I can hardly wait. I know they'll all be wonderful."

An icy wind pushed David home from school.

When Dad got home, Sarah reached for the candle box, "My turn to light the candles," she said.

"No, I'm lighting the candles tonight," David said, pulling the box away from her. The box flew open and rainbow colored candles scattered all over the carpet.

"Since tonight is the last night of Hanukkah, we'll *all* light the candles," Mom decided.

The wind rattled the windows as they lit the eight candles. The tiny flames flickered.

"It's cold in here," Susan said with a shiver. "Can we make a fire in the fireplace?"

David pulled on his jacket and cap and stepped outside to fetch some wood.

Across the street, strings of bright white lights clung to a pair of spruce trees. Red, green, and yellow lights outlined the house next door. The lights from town glowed on the horizon. In David's front window, his family's silhouettes shimmered in the Hanukkah candlelight. Stars spilled across the sky. The world seemed filled with tiny lights, all different and all shining. David picked up the wood and hurried inside.

"Today we'll hear your stories," Miss Wagner said. "Who wants to go first?"

One by one, David's classmates stood up and read their stories: stories about everything from Midnight Mass and caroling in the snow to big family dinners and bright Christmas mornings.

Then it was David's turn. He stood up and stared at the page in front of him.

"My, uh...my...my f-fav...er...favorite...um...my...Oh, I don't really have a favorite Christmas. My family doesn't celebrate Christmas. We celebrate Hanukkah. Everyone knows about Christmas, but not everyone knows about Hanukkah."

The class listened closely as David told them about the Maccabees and the oil, about the *menorah*, the candles, the songs, and the *dreydel* game. When he told them about Mom's potato *latkes* and Uncle Morris's chocolate *gelt,* Dennis licked his lips. By the time he finished, Jimmy was spinning an invisible *dreydel.* Nancy wanted to learn a Hannukah song. Miss Wagner was smiling. And David's face shone like a candle flame dancing in a frosty window.

Polly's Frippery
by Andrea Spalding

It happened last year, on a wet November day when I visited Hycroft House, an old mansion in the heart of Vancouver. Hycroft House is usually a club where university women, like my mom, hang out to play bridge games and attend lectures—but once a year it's magical! Each November Hycroft is decorated and opened to the public for a Christmas sale. Every room is transformed with hundreds of ornaments, Christmas trees, wreaths, lights, and dried flowers. Mom and I always volunteer to work at a booth. We both wear old-fashioned dresses and sweep around like duchesses.

I help Mom, bagging Christmas cookies and tying them with fancy ribbons. I work fast so when I'm finished I can spend time searching for my special ornament. Every year I save money to buy the nicest Christmas ornament in the display. I spend ages choosing it, then I add it to my collection.

I climbed halfway up the big curved staircase, and sat tucked against the balustrade, nibbling on a broken cookie, watching the crowds, and deciding where to start my ornament search. The mansion smelled like Christmas...cedar, baking, mulled cider and potpourri, and people were laughing and talking over the Christmas music. I found myself imagining that this was my mansion and I was related to the McRaes, the first family who owned Hycroft in the early 1900s.

It was a splendid daydream. I was a McRae daughter with jewels, money, servants, and a horse and carriage of my own, and all the people milling around were guests invited to the masquerade ball my family held each year.

I only snapped out of the daydream when I spotted another girl coming up the stairs!

Now I thought my dress was pretty authentic, but this girl was totally in character. She wore the perfect copy of an old-fashioned maid's uniform, a calf-length black dress with starched apron and a little mob cap, like a white cotton shower cap with a frill around the edge, perched on her head. She looked wonderful.

I grinned. "Ah Polly," I said, "make me a cup of tea," expecting her to laugh.

She looked at me sternly. "No food outside the dining-room, miss," she replied, in a great Northern English accent. Then she glared at my hand curled around the banister rail, "...and don't put them sticky fingers on the banister....I were up at five this morning polishing." She took the corner of her apron and gave the rail a good rub.

I was flabbergasted....I thought *I* could role play; this girl was brilliant.

"Great outfit. Here, have a broken cookie...." I fished another out of my pocket.

She shrank back and looked uncomfortable. That's when I realized I could faintly see through her.

"Holy guacamole! You're a *ghost*!"

"Shssssh." She placed her finger on her lips and I looked around. Luckily the noise level was so high that no one had heard my exclamation.

"My name, miss. 'Ow did you know it?" she asked.

"I didn't...it was your outfit and the old nursery rhyme." I sang it for her softly, "Polly put the kettle on, we'll all have tea." Polly smiled in recognition.

"Er...I'm Melanie Roberts. Am I the only person that can see and hear you?"

Polly nodded shyly.

"Can we go somewhere and talk? I've never met a ghost before. "

Polly climbed the steps to the second floor. I followed, through a doorway and into a narrow corridor.

"Up 'ere," whispered Polly, and drifted up a twisty dusty staircase.

"Where are we going?"

"To the servants' quarters. Me room's in the attic. General McRae liked us servants out of the way."

Polly wasn't scary, she was just a girl like me, but that

staircase and attic corridor were. I don't do narrow, dark and dusty. I half expected something nasty to leap out of each closed wooden door we passed.

Polly's room was tiny and tucked under the slope of the roof with only enough height to stand upright by the door. I stood in the middle bit with two L-shaped sections, on either side of me, each going out to a dormer window. The room was like a capital letter E without the middle bar. Polly sat on the beat-up remains of a narrow metal bed in the left hand section.

The attic was freezing. I shivered.

"'Ere, sit against me radiator," Polly suggested.

I hadn't noticed the tiny hot water radiator on the wall beside her bed. Its metal was molded into curls and swirls. I traced them with my finger. It was barely warm.

"I was the lucky kitchen maid, 'aving that radiator. My mate Sarah almost froze to death under the other window. You 'ave to lean against it mind, or the 'eat don't reach," Polly said. "Go on, I don't feel 'ot or cold in my present state."

I sat beside her on a faded and torn quilt, stuck my back against the radiator and tucked my feet under my skirt. "So, tell me, why are you haunting this place? Did the McRaes murder you?"

Polly looked scornful. "Don't be daft," she said forthrightly.

"Besides, I don't haunt nothin'. I just like to visit once a year...for the Christmas celebration."

"WHY?"

Polly looked dreamy-eyed. "My family was poor. But I worked 'ere...and for once I was going to enjoy a real Christmas. Us servants talked of nothin' else. The McRaes gave proper presents see. Even to the under-maids and the gardener's boys."

"What do you mean, 'proper presents'?"

Polly laughed. "Not summat useful like a pair of shoes, or a new apron. I was promised a frippery."

"I don't get it. What's a frippery?"

"You know...a bauble...a gewgaw....summat pretty but not very useful." She gestured towards the floor. "Hycroft's full of 'em down below."

"You mean like the Christmas balls and wreaths?"

Polly nodded. "Ooh, I was that excited. My family 'ad only emigrated from England a few months earlier. Times 'ad been bad after the war, and me dad hadn't worked since he'd got discharged from the army. We came to Canada hoping for work here."

"What year was it?" I asked.

"End of the world war, silly, 1918." Polly snorted. "But finding jobs weren't much better 'ere, till me mum landed work at the fish cannery."

"I visited a cannery on a school trip."

Polly shuddered. "What do you want to go there for? They're 'orrible places. Stinking noisy holes, full of rotting fish and dangerous machinery."

I said nothing. I'd seen a clean, tidy, and pretty boring warehouse.

"Then me mum 'eard General McRae needed a

kitchen maid."

"How did she hear about the McRaes at the fish cannery?" I asked, puzzled.

"McRaes owned it. Me dad was sick and me mum right pleased I'd landed a job in service. Me wages meant they could eat a bit extra and look for two rooms to rent instead of all six of 'em living in one. So I came to live here."

"Lucky you," I said enviously. "This is my favorite house in the world."

"You've got rocks in your head," Polly replied. "You should try lighting fires at five in the morning, scrubbing steps in the freezing cold, peeling 'undreds of spuds or carrots, cleaning up everyone else's muck, and being yelled at by the whole flippin' lot."

"What about school?"

"What about it? I was twelve. We needed money, not learnin' in our family." She paused sadly. "Wish I could have 'elped me Mum longer."

I felt guilty. I was the same age as Polly but I couldn't imagine helping support my family. "What happened?"

"Well...I'd gone over the road to the kitchen garden to fetch Cook a basket full of vegetables. I was feeling ill. My head 'urt, my feet felt like lead, and the basket was so heavy my arms were nearly pulled out of their sockets. I'd just started back when I 'eard a right ruckus...men shouting and hollerin', and the sound of hooves and wagon wheels. A horse had been spooked by one of them automobiles. I turned to run out of the way, but me head went all woozy and I fainted just as the runaway horse and wagon rounded the corner."

I shuddered and shut my eyes, then felt a touch like icy feathers on my arm.

"It's all right Melanie, it happened so fast I don't remember even hurtin'. It were no one's fault." Polly paused and sighed. "But I did wish I'd 'ad one real Christmas."

I stood up. "Come on then. Let's have Christmas together."

We left the room. I nervously crept down the stairs, along the passage, and peeked around the doorway. No one was there.

I drew myself up and shook out my dress. "Right," I said to Polly.

"Try using YOUR imagination. I'm young Miss McRae, and you're my best friend and we're going to the Masquerade Ball."

Polly giggled.

"Instead of your uniform, you're wearing...a green velvet dress...with a pearl necklace...and...and a matching velvet bow in your hair."

Polly giggled again. "The likes of me don't dress as gentry."

"Concentrate Polly... a dress as green as the cedars... as warm as a wool blanket...but as soft as goosedown."

And there she stood in a beautiful green velvet party dress, with a string of pearls, a fur muff hanging from a cord around her neck, and a pair of shiny gold slippers on her feet.

"Cor blimey. I always fancied these," she said as she surveyed her shoes with satisfaction, and tucked her hands inside the muff.

We swept down the stairs with confidence and joined the noisy throng of shoppers.

"Deck the halls with boughs of holly," sang the carolers.

"Fa la la la la, la la la la," warbled Polly happily. She was off key, but only I could hear. We edged through the crowd to admire the Christmas trees. One was covered with gold ornaments, and one full of birds. A scarlet bow tree caught our eye, and the teddy bears' tree made us smile. Then we saw the silver tree. Polly stopped and quivered with delight.

"Smashing, i'n' it? That's like the McRaes." And she stood in a trance.

The silver tree grew brighter and brighter and the surroundings hazier. I started to feel apprehensive, then realized Polly was remembering her long ago Christmas and magically showing me.

I gasped. For the whole room subtly shifted and changed. The tree shimmered in a halo of light from a hundred candles clipped to its branch tips. The candle-light danced and sparkled over a room full, not of shoppers, but of shadowy people in fancy dress. I recognized General and Mrs. McRae from the old Hycroft photos I'd seen. Dressed in Turkish costumes they greeted masquerading friends. A gaily-coloured Harlequin escorted his full-skirted Columbine, Henry the VIII and Anne Boleyn nodded to a kimono-clad Japanese noblemen and geisha and clowns, veiled princesses and knights in armour gathered in throngs throughout the room. Everyone held cocktails and laughed and chatted while waiting for the McRaes fabled masquerade ball to commence.

Suddenly dance music drifted up from the ballroom and two by two the colorful but ghostly party-goers floated past us and headed down to the ballroom to circle around the floor in a lively quickstep.

Servants entered the empty room and began setting up a gigantic party buffet.

"Goodness, how did they appear?" I asked.

"Secret passages," explained Polly. "Little corridors 'idden behind walls. General and Mrs. McRae didn't like seeing us servants, so they made passages behind the main rooms of the mansion." She chuckled. "Gosh, we scuttered out of their way fast. Christmas was really the only time they ever met us lower servants...to give us our gifts."

As Polly talked, the scene subtly shifted. A stiff line of servants stood uncomfortably beside the tree. General McRae quickly shook each servant's hand and they bobbed a curtsy or bow. Mrs. McRae handed each of them a small but beautifully wrapped gift. The servants murmured their thanks, then silently filed out.

The scene from the past faded away and we were once again surrounded by a cheerful throng of modern shoppers.

"That was it?" That was how you would have received your gift?"

Polly nodded.

I felt horrible, upset and angry, and glad I wasn't a servant.

"Polly, has a friend never given you a present?"

She shook her head.

"Well I'm going to give you one. If you could choose anything you liked off this tree, what would you pick?"

Polly gazed intently at the beautiful decorations then pointed to a branch halfway up. A delicate silver-and-white bauble spun slowly. It was covered with glass beads that sparkled and shimmered with rainbow facets; from its base hung a pear-shaped crystal. It was the prettiest decoration I had ever seen. We both gazed in admiration.

I took Polly's hand, led her over to the fireside and we knelt down on the rug. "Polly, it's imagination time again." I held my hands out in front of me. "Here's your present."

Polly looked at my empty hands in astonishment.

"Come on Polly, imagine....It's a beautiful gift for you...I've wrapped it in gold paper...with a scarlet satin ribbon... and a sprig of holly on the top."

And there, cupped in my hands, glowed a small gold package just exactly as I had described. "Take it Polly... it's yours."

Gently Polly lifted the box and sat with it on her lap, stroking the ribbon and running her fingers over the foil paper. Then slowly, oh so slowly, she unwrapped it.

First gold paper, then a white box filled with crinkly white tissue, then delicately she lifted out the beaded Christmas ornament. It glittered in the firelight and the crystal drop matched a tear trembling on her lashes.

"Thank you, thank you, Melanie, you're the kindest, cleverest friend I ever 'ad." She leaned forward, dropped a kiss like a snowflake on my cheek, and vanished.

Just like that, she was gone!

Shaken, I got to my feet, wondering if I'd let my imagination get the better of me.

I wandered slowly back to the silver tree and looked at it again. It was beautiful, though not quite as spectacular as my memory of the McRaes tree shimmering with candles.

Never mind, it was the best tree at Hycroft that year and I would buy the beautiful silver-and-white ornament in memory of Polly.

I looked for the branch...surely it was that one... right there...but the branch that once held Polly's frippery was empty!

Historical Notes and Author Biographies

The Crosscut

After coal was discovered on Vancouver Island in 1848, many mining towns materialized to supply homes and services for workers and their families. The mines were below both ground and ocean and were wet, dark and dangerous. Often mine owners and administrators did not obey the safety requirements needed to protect their workers. Boys were not officially allowed to work in the mine until they were sixteen. In British Columbia, many Chinese immigrants worked in the mines and were often the subject of racist segregation and abuse, some seen as scapegoats wrongly blamed for mine accidents. This racism was a reflection of an overall attitude toward the Chinese in B.C. during this time period. Mining in Nanaimo ended in 1953 and on the rest of the Island in 1965.

Lynne Bowen is the author of *Boss Whistle: The Coal Miners of Vancouver Island Remember* (Oolichan, 1982), *Three Dollar Dreams* (Oolichan, 1987), *The Dunsmuirs of Nanaimo* (Nanaimo Festival, 1989), *Muddling Through: The Remarkable Story of the Barr Colonists*

(Douglas & McIntyre, 1992) and *Those Lake People: Stories of Cowichan Lake* (Douglas & McIntyre, 1995). She has won numerous awards for her historical non-fiction work and has also written for radio, video and magazines. She lives in Nanaimo, B.C. where, on occasion, she gives coal mining tours.

On Manson Creek

The tale of Sing and Emma is a true story recorded in the Aural Archives of British Columbia and related by Wiggs O'Neill. In the 1920 the Grand Trunk Pacific Railway (now the CPR) travelled this route from Vanderhoof to Prince Rupert. At that time Mr. Tim Chow and George Chuey ran the O.K. Café on Stewart St. in Vanderhoof (and continued to do so for twenty-two years), charging fifty cents for meals. From the northern mining camps of the Omineca Gold Rush, men would come to the area for meals and accommodation while waiting for spring break-up. Gold was first discovered in the Omineca River region, including Mason Creek, in 1869. The rush to stake gold claims peaked in 1871.

Joan Skogan's work has been read on numerous CBC radio programs and has appeared in *Saturday Night, The Georgia Straight, Border Crossings* and many daily newspapers and literary magazines. Her books in print include *The Good Companion* (Orca, 1998), *Voyages at Sea with Strangers* (HarperCollins, 1992),

Grey Cat at Sea (Polestar, 1991), *The Princess and the Sea Bear and Other Tsimshian Stories* (Polestar, 1992) and *Skeena: A River Remembered* (B.C. Heritage, 1983). Her stories have appeared in *North Coast Collected, Shorelines: The Discovery Islands Anthology, Canadian Children's Annual, Share a Tale* and other anthologies. She has taught adults in various schools and has worked in the commercial fishing industry. She lives on Gabriola Island, B.C.

Measuring Up

Walhachin is an orchard settlement that was created in the middle of the desert by a hundred or so inexperienced men and women newly immigrated from England. When the first World War arrived the men of this flourishing community returned to Europe to fight for the Allies. For three years the women managed to keep the orchard alive, but the spring of 1917 freak storm washed out the supports of the twenty-mile water flume that provided essential irrigation for the fruit trees leaving them to wither and die. When the war ended the men stayed on in England where jobs were now plentiful and the women deserted Walhachin to join them.

Joan Weir is the author of twelve novels for young adult readers and six non-fiction Canadian histories including *Catalysts & Watchdogs: B.C.'s Men of God* (Sono Nis, 1995), *Backdoor to the Klondike* (Boston

Mills, 1988) and *Walhachin: Catastrophe or Camelot* (Hancock House, 1984). Her novels include *The Witcher* (Polestar, 1998), *Brideship* (Stoddart, 1998), *Mystery at Lighthouse Rock* (Stoddart, 1991), *Say Yes* (Greey de Pencier, 1991), *Secret Ballot* (Greey de Pencier, 1991), *Ski Lodge Mystery* (Stoddart, 1988), *Balloon Race Mystery* (Stoddart, 1988), *Sixteen is Spelled O-U-C-H* (Stoddart, 1988), *Storm Rider* (Scholastic, 1988), *Secret at Westwind* (Scholastic, 1981) and *So, I'm Different* (Douglas & McIntyre, 1981). Joan lives and teaches in Kamloops, B.C.

A Hero's Welcome

In late 1945 armed service personnel returned from World War II to their families in the homes they had left more than four years before. Many men had difficulty readjusting to their wives and children after such a long separation. Children had grown, wives had gone to work or disappeared and returning men felt at loose ends, unwanted, bitter, and resentful. One historical account of a returning soldier tells the story of a father who found fault with everything his son had done on the farm without a single word of praise. That account became the basis for this story.

Barbara Haworth-Attard is the author of *Home Child* (Roussan, 1996), *Truthsinger* (Roussan, 1996), *The Three Wishbells* (Roussan, 1995) and *Dark of the Moon*

(Roussan, 1994). Her work has been shortlisted for the Mr. Christie Award, has been a *Resource Links* "Year's Best" and a Canadian Children's Book Centre "Our Choice" winner. Her own father fought in World War II but never spoke of the war at all. After his death in 1994, his children discovered suitcases full of war memorabilia, letters he'd written home and medals, all of which also helped to inspire this story. Barbara Haworth-Attard now lives in London, Ontario.

Grampus

The Fisgard lighthouse was built in 1860 to help ships find their way into Esquimalt Harbour, an important naval base west of Victoria on Vancouver Island. It is preserved as part of Fort Rodd Hill historic park. Fisgard's first keeper and his family came from Britain, bringing the new light apparatus made near Birmingham. What the boys witness in the story has happened; transient orcas *do* attack seals. Whaling was carried out in the Victoria area during this period. Whales were not well understood, and Bell's *History of British Quadrupeds* might well have been used to interpret a transient Orca's attack on a seal.

David Spalding is a writer and editor of several books, many scripts, and hundreds of articles. He has lived in England and Alberta, and now on Pender Island, B.C. He is a geologist and naturalist who writes about nature, particularly dinosaurs. He has contributed to science textbooks, won awards for educational radio, and hosted television series. With his wife Andrea Spalding, he has written several books (see biography of Andrea Spalding for titles), and performed as a folk musician and storyteller. This is his first published fiction.

The Harmonica

From the late 1800s to the outbreak of the second World War in 1939, many orphans in Britain were sent to families in North America where they could learn various trades. These children were sometimes called 'Home Children.' Some of the families they went to stay with, lived on farms in Canada where the children became valued members of the family. But some were badly mistreated by their 'masters' and used any means of escape, only to be dragged back again to their unhappy life on the farm. Shortly after the war, a particularly lethal strain of influenza struck people in Europe and America so that more people died of this horrible epidemic than in the entire four years of the Great War.

Norma Charles is the author of *Dolphin Alert* (Nelson, 1998), *Darlene's Shadow* (General, 1991), *April Fool Heroes* (Nelson, 1990), *No Place for a Horse* (General, 1988), *Amanda Grows Up* (Scholastic, 1978) and *See You Later, Alligator* (Scholastic, 1976). Her story "Lum King's Horse" appeared in *How I Learned to*

Speak Dog. Norma Charles was a teacher-librarian for ten years, but now devotes herself full-time to writing and giving readings and writing workshops. She lives in Vancouver, B.C. and teaches Writing For Children at UBC.

The Scarlatina

A wave of Health Reform swept across North America between the 1840s and 1870s in reaction to doctors' tendencies to prescribe large doses of alcohol or drugs as cures for largely misunderstood diseases. Some Reformers subscribed to a popular type of alternative medicine called the "water cure", which maintained that pure water could cure almost any disease. These Reformers also believed that women should wear clothing that was loose and practical to permit better circulation. Dr. Russell Thatcher Trall's *The Hydropathic Encyclopedia* contained information on the water cure and was used by thousands in treating sickness at home. Some Protestant Christians saw the method as "natural" and therefore part of "God's will" while disease was an evil force controlled by the Devil. Thus, more fanatical health reformers saw the struggle against disease as a kind of holy crusade. Although attempts to heal with water failed, a doctor of the day had no better cure for scarlet fever.

Joanne Findon's great-grandmother was a water cure fanatic in her youth, and lost two of her youngest children to scarlet fever. She recorded her extreme behaviour in the hope that her children would learn from her mistakes. Joanne Findon is the author of *The Dream of Aengus* (Stoddart, 1994), *Auld Lang Syne* (Stoddart, 1997) and has had stories appear in *Takes, The Blue Jean Collection, Cycles 1* and the *Canadian Children's Annual.* She reviews children's books for many publications and lives in Surrey, B.C.

A Horse for Lisette

The Red River Settlement was established by the Scottish Lord Selkirk in 1811, in the valleys of the Red and Assiniboine Rivers. This settlement was close to the present site of Winnipeg, Manitoba. During the 1800s, there was a growing population of "mixed blood" children, known as Metis. They were the offspring of French Canadian voyageurs who transferred furs between the isolated trading posts and Native women. Men from England and Scotland who came to the west to work these posts wanted Metis girls as wives because they had all the skills of their Native mothers yet could adapt to the white culture. Fathers offered daughters in marriage, often as young as twelve, to these British men believing it would not only raise their daughters' status, but would also bring more class to their own household. The girls' consent was not essential.

Linda Holeman is the author of several books for young adults and children including *Promise Song* (Tundra, 1997), *Frankie on the Run* (Boardwalk Books, 1995) and *Saying Good-bye* (Lester, 1995). She has also written an adult short story collection: *Flying to Yellow* (Turnstone, 1996). She has a young adult title forthcoming from Tundra in the fall of 1998 and another adult story collection to debut from Porcupine's Quill in 1999. Her stories have been anthologized in *The Journey Prize Anthology*, *Due West: Great Stories from Alberta, Saskatchewan and Manitoba*, *Notes Across the Aisle*, *Success Stories for the '90s* and *The Blue Jean Collection*. Her adult fiction and poetry has appeared in numerous literary magazines. She lives in Winnipeg, Manitoba.

Higher Ground

In 1914, with the help of Nellie McClung, Canadian women earned the right to vote. McClung was also one of the "famous five," who in 1929 led the legal challenge to have women declared persons thereby making them eligible for office as Canadian senators. Our Nell handled all her roles capably—legislator, lecturer, teacher, writer, wife and mother. Although she didn't begin school until she was ten years old, she had a way with words which, combined with courage and a respect for humanity, made her a powerful leader. She died in 1951, leaving Canada a different place than she had found it.

Beverly Brenna is the author of *Spider Summer* (Nelson, 1997) and *Daddy Long Legs at Birch Lane* (The Smithsonian, 1996). Her stories and poetry have appeared in *Takes, bite to eat place* and *Do Whales Sing at Night?*. She has won a number of awards from the Saskatchewan Writer's Guild and has had work published in various magazines and newspapers. She lives in Saskatoon, Saskatchewan.

Wolves and Heathens

Although this story is fictionalized, it is based on an actual flight made by Jimmy "Midnight" Anderson of Mile 147, Alaska Highway, Pink Mountain, B.C. who made some legendary flights in his Super Cub. Bush pilots during this period explored some of Canada's most unforgiving country and often rescued people and animals stranded on islands in the middle of raging rivers, lost deep in the mountains, trapped on the tundra or caught in a forest fire. Military and commercial flyers embodied the pioneer spirit and brought people together by allowing access to and from vast wilderness areas. A story about Jimmy's life as a bush pilot is chronicled in "The Jackpine Savage," *Flying the Frontiers Vol. I* also by Shirlee Smith Matheson.

Shirlee Smith Matheson is the author of *The Gambler's Daughter* (Beach Holme, 1997), *Prairie Pictures* (McClelland & Stewart, 1990), *Flying Ghosts*

(Stoddart, 1993) and *City Pictures* (McClelland & Stewart, 1994). She is the author of several non-fiction works including *Youngblood of the Peace* (Detselig, 1991), *This Was Our Valley* (Detselig Enterprises, 1989), *Flying the Frontiers* (Fifth House, 1994), *Flying the Frontiers Volume II* (Detselig Enterprises, 1996) and *A Western Welcome to the World* (Cheribo, 1997). Matheson also publishes short stories and plays and frequently gives readings and workshops in schools and libraries. She currently lives in Calgary, Alberta.

Where There's Smoke

Early Canadian settlers made cheese for their own use and for sale at farmer's markets. The first factory specializing in making cheese from milk supplied by district farmers was built in Oxford County, Ontario in 1863. By 1900 there were 2300 cheese factories in Canada, mostly in Ontario and Quebec. Mammoth cheeses were made for promotion purposes. The "Canadian Mite", made in Perth, Ontario of Canadian cheddar, weighed ten tons and was displayed in Chicago and then in London, England. In *Reminiscences of a Canadian Pioneer* by Samuel Thompson, (McClelland & Stewart, 1968) the author tells about an insurance inspector investigating the claim of the owner of a cheese factory fraudulently destroyed by fire. His clue to the hoax was the fact that the cheese burned without a smell.

Constance Horne is the author of *The Accidental Orphan* (Beach Holme, 1998), *Emily Carr's Woo* (Oolichan, 1995), *Trapped by Coal* (Pacific Educational, 1994), *The Jo Boy Deserts and Other Stories* (Pacific Educational, 1992) and *Nykola and Granny* (Gage, 1989). Her books have been chosen by the Canadian Children's Book Centre as "Our Choice" award winners and she has been short-listed three times for the Geoffrey Bilson Award. She taught school for several years and now lives in Victoria, British Columbia.

Shadows of the Past

The southern Gulf Islands lie stretched along the coast of Vancouver Island between Nanaimo and Victoria. The first European settlers arrived in the 1850s and established farms which for many years supplied Victoria with much of its fresh produce. These settlers were followed by disillusioned gold miners, African-Americans from California, Hawaiian islanders and Japanese Canadians. Market gardening, fishing, salting and seaweed harvesting were common occupations for those islanders in addition to pole cutting needed to supply supports for the coal mines in Nanaimo and Cumberland. The Gulf Islands maintain the diversity in heritage and talent of those first settlers to this day.

John Wilson's novels *Weet* (Napoleon, 1995), *Weet's Quest* (Napoleon, 1997) and *Across Frozen Seas* (Beach

Holme, 1997) have made him popular for readings and presentations to school children from Grades 4 to 8. Wilson is currently working on an adult work on the Franklin Expedition and a young adult novel set in the Spanish Civil War. He has taught writing at Malaspina College in Nanaimo and the University of Victoria. In 1986 he travelled around the world, freelancing travel and feature journalism articles and photo essays.

Remember, Chrysanthemum

In 1942, approximately 21,000 men, women and children of Japanese descent were forced to leave the West Coast of British Columbia to go to interment camps, labour farms and road camps. By April 1949, Japanese Canadians received the right to vote and to move anywhere in Canada. Negotiations between the National Association of Japanese Canadians and the Government of Canada resulted in Conservative Prime Minister Brian Mulroney's formal apology to the Japanese Canadians on September 22, 1988. The resultant redress settlement compensated the Japanese community and individual survivors.

Kathryn Hatashita-Lee was born in Toronto and grew up in Vancouver, B.C. She attended the University of British Columbia and Emily Carr Institute of Art and Design where she studied history and photography. "Remember, Chrysanthemum" is her first published story.

One Candle, Many Lights

Following the Great Depression in the thirties, World War II and post-war austerity in the forties, the fifties introduced vast changes and growth. An event that marked the period for Canadians was the day seventeen year old Marilyn Bell, against nearly impossible odds, became the first person to swim across Lake Ontario. She also went on to become the youngest to swim the English Channel. In a small town like Lone Butte in British Columbia's central interior, children like David and his sisters would have heard about Bell's success and seen her determination as an inspiration for future generations of young Canadians. Such courage was similarly evident when David stood before his classmates and shared his Jewish faith and culture in a community which assumed all its members were Christian. This too was a victory of sorts.

Kathleen Cook Waldron grew up in the United States before immigrating with her family to the Cariboo region of British Columbia. She has taught on both sides of the border, but now devotes most of her time to writing. Her work in print includes four picture books: *A Winter's Yarn* (Red Deer College, 1986), *A Wilderness Passover* (Red Deer College, 1994), *Ivan and the All-Stars* (Boardwalk Books, 1995) and *The Loon Lake Fishing Derby* (Orca, 1998). Her story "Dill Pickles" appears in the anthology *Jumbo Gumbo* (Coteau, 1989). She lives in 100 Mile House, B.C.

Polly's Frippery

Beautiful Hycroft House is a real place in Vancouver. Built in 1909 for the McRae family, it was considered Vancouver's finest mansion. Tales of the McRae's lavish dinners and their fabled masquerade balls still circulate; so do rumours of their disdain for servants. The secret passages and cramped attic quarters are now used for storage, but they still contrast sharply with the opulent main rooms and beautiful ballroom. Currently owned by the University Women's Club, Hycroft is opened to the public each November for 'Christmas At Hycroft,' a sale to raise funds for charities. Polly is fictional, but it is likely that at least one servant at Hycroft would have died during the flu epidemic that raged through Vancouver in 1918.

Andrea Spalding is an editor, musician, actress, professional storyteller, and writer for radio and television. Brandywine, her folk duo, has produced two records: "Breakfast with Brandywine" and "The Most Beautiful Kite in the World." She has co-authored *Superguide to the Southern Gulf Islands* (Altitude, 1995), *The Flavours of Victoria* (Orca, 1994), *The Pender Palate* (Loon Books, 1992), *The Whistlers* (Jasper National Park, 1986), *Never a Dull Moment* (Collins, 1984). She is the sole author of *A World of Stories* (Red Deer, 1989), *The Most Beautiful Kite in the World* (Red Deer, 1988) and *Finders Keepers* (Beach Holme, 1995). Spalding also co-wrote a TV series on Alberta ethnic groups, "Through Western Eyes." She lives on Pender Island, British Columbia where she operates a bed and breakfast with her husband, author David Spalding.

Ann Walsh is the author of *Shabash!* (Beach Holme, 1994), *Ghost of Soda Creek* (Beach Holme, 1990), *Across the Stillness* (Beach Holme, 1992), *Moses, Me and Murder* (Pacific Educational, 1988) and *Your Time, My Time* (Beach Holme, 1984). She has been nominated for the Silver Birch Award and is a Canadian Children's Book Centre "Our Choice" award winner. Her work has also appeared in *The Blue Jean Collection, Great Canadian Murders & Mysteries* and *The Skin of the Soul*. She has published articles in journals in Sweden, Canada and the United States. Ann Walsh lives in Williams Lake, B.C.